GUARDIANS OF CLACHANOCH

DEE WHITMAN

GUARDIANS OF CLACHANOCH

CONTENTS

PROLOGUE

Echoes of Clachanoch

The Highland moors, wrapped in their eternal mist, murmured secrets to those who dared to listen. In the early hours of dawn, when the world was still and the air was thick with the scent of heather, Dougal McBeth jolted awake, his breath fogging in the chill air of the croft. His skin prickled with cold sweat, and his heart pounded like hooves on stone. Outside, the Highland mist coiled thick across the moors—but it wasn't the weather that had woken him. It was Clachanoch.

In his dreams, the estate had stood proud against the rugged landscape, its towering stone walls sheltering the echoes of long-gone voices. He wandered its grand halls, his footsteps a ghostly whisper against polished floors, and watched candlelight dance across tapestries woven with the triumphs and tragedies of his ancestors. The estate, once a beacon of prestige and honour, now lay in ruins, its legacy fading with the passage of time.

As dawn's first light crept through the curtains, Dougal sat up slowly, still caught in the gravity of his dream. The vivid images lingered in his mind, not merely dreams but a summons. Clachanoch was more than an ancestral relic—it was a calling, a responsibility waiting to be reclaimed.

Turning to his wife, Maree, he shared his visions, his voice edged with an urgency he could scarcely explain. Maree, ever his steadfast companion, listened intently. She had always known of Dougal's deep connection to the Highland moors, the whispers of the past threading through their shared dreams. Now, with Clachanoch beckoning, the pull of history felt stronger than ever.

"We must go, Maree," he said, his voice firm as the Highland winds. "We must see the estate with our own eyes and uncover the truths hidden within its walls."

Maree's gaze met his, unwavering. "Aye, Dougal. If the estate calls tae ye, then we shall heed its call. But we dinnae walk alone—we should speak tae the others."

The decision weighed heavily between them, but it felt inevitable—as if the land itself had laid this path before their feet. Maree moved to the window and parted the curtain. Mist still rolled over the moors like breath over still waters, and somewhere in that silence, she felt the echo of the estate's heartbeat calling them onward.

Dougal reached for the satchel where he kept the map of the Highlands, spreading it across the kitchen table. His fingers hovered over the region where Clachanoch lay, a faded ink mark barely visible. "We'll need supplies... and answers," he murmured. "There are things I need to ken before I set foot in that place again."

"Then we begin quietly," Maree said. "A visit. Just us. We walk the ruins. We listen. We ask the land what it wants from us."

Dougal nodded. "Aye. An' if the moors speak as they have before, we'll follow. But first—we listen."

When they gathered with their kin and closest friends later that day, the notion of a journey to Clachanoch stirred a mix of intrigue and uncertainty. It was then that Fiona spoke, her voice low yet brimming with significance.

"The dream I had last night—aye, it was Clachanoch... but not as it stands now. In ma dream, we walked its halls no' as visitors tae a ruin, but as those who belonged tae another time. The estate was alive, grand an' opulent, its chandeliers ablaze wi' light, the scent o' fine perfumes an' aged brandy thick in the air. But beneath the splendour, I felt somethin' darker—secrets buried beneath layers o' silk an' stone, an' a presence watchin' from the shadows."

A hush fell over the room. Elspeth, the guardian of the Highland moors, folded her hands over her lap, her keen eyes glinting with knowledge unspoken. "The heart o' Clachanoch Estate doesnae rest in its stones alone," she murmured. "It lies within its past, within the choices o' those who walked afore ye. To return is not merely to reclaim what was lost, but to uncover what has long been hidden. What lies buried at Clachanoch may nae just shape yer past," she added softly, "but change what's still tae come."

A weight settled over Dougal, a mingling of anticipation and foreboding. This was no simple homecoming. If Fiona's dream held truth, they would not merely step into a ruin—they would step into history itself, into an era of grandeur and deception, where alliances were made and broken under flickering candlelight, and where power was wielded not only by steel but by whispered words and unseen hands.

The Highland winds stirred outside, carrying with them the voices of the past.

Together, they would embark on a journey to Clachanoch, not just to restore a legacy—but to face the ghosts that still walked its halls.

LIFE AT CLACHANOCH ESTATE

The first light of dawn crept through the tall, mullioned windows of the nursery at Clachanoch Estate, gently waking eleven-year-old Fyonna McBeth. She rubbed her eyes and sat up, greeted by the faint glow of morning that danced along the stone walls. In the next bed, her brother Alistair—just a year older at twelve—pulled the covers over his head with a sleepy groan, reluctant to surrender the last moments of slumber.

Morven MacTavish, the children's devoted nanny, was already bustling about the nursery with practised ease. Dressed in a neat grey morning dress and crisp white apron, she moved between their beds carrying a basin of warm water. "Come now, my wee ones," she said warmly, her lilting Highland accent soft in the quiet room. "Time to rise. The Laird and Lady will be expecting ye downstairs shortly."

At the sound of Morven's voice, Fyonna smiled and swung her legs out of bed, the cool wood floor under her feet prompting a quick shiver. Morven set the basin on a washstand and helped Fyonna wash her face and hands. The water was scented lightly with lavender—Lady Isobel's own touch, ensuring the children's day began with a bit of gentle comfort. As Morven brushed out Fyonna's long dark hair, she hummed an old Gaelic lullaby under her breath, a tune that had welcomed many a morning in this nursery. Fyonna closed her eyes briefly, enjoying the familiar melody and the tender care in Morven's touch.

Across the room, Alistair was still burrowed in his blankets. Morven clicked her tongue and gave a playful tug at the thick quilt. "Up with ye, a bhobain," she chided affectionately, using a Gaelic endearment as she patted the lump that was Alistair. "We've a full day ahead, Master Alistair. Your father will be wanting to see you bright-eyed at breakfast."

With a dramatic sigh, Alistair finally emerged, his brown hair sticking in all directions. He tried to stifle a yawn as Morven guided him to the washstand. Fyonna, already dressed in a clean blue day frock with a white pinafore, grinned at her brother's sleepy face. "Ye look like a ruffl'd owl," she teased quietly. Alistair made a face at her in the mirror, but the corners of his mouth twitched in a smile.

Despite the early hour, there was a comforting rhythm to these mornings that even he secretly enjoyed.

Morven soon had Alistair washed and neatly dressed in a pressed tweed knickerbocker suit appropriate for a young heir of a Highland estate. She gave his hair a final smoothing with her hand, inspecting both children to be sure they were presentable. The nanny's pride in her charges shone in her eyes as she straightened Fyonna's collar and brushed an imaginary speck of dust from Alistair's shoulder.

"All right, me dears, doon we go," Morven said, ushering them toward the nursery door. Fyonna took Alistair's hand as they followed her out into the corridor. The hallway was still quiet at this hour, but the household was beginning to stir. The scent of baking bread drifted from the kitchens downstairs, and somewhere in the distance they heard a stable door opening with a low creak—likely one of the grooms starting his morning tasks with the horses.

As they descended the grand oak staircase, the grandeur of Clachanoch House emerged gradually around them. Early sunlight streamed through the landing's stained-glass window, which depicted the McBeth clan crest—a silver stag on a field of blue—and cast dappled colours onto the marble floor below. Fyonna and Alistair had passed that majestic window every morning of their lives; today, as always, it filled them with a quiet sense of pride and belonging.

At the foot of the stairs, Agnes Sinclair, the housekeeper, awaited with a fond smile. Agnes was a stately woman with iron-grey hair pulled back in a bun and a face that often seemed stern to outsiders. But the children knew better—many a time had they been secretly slipped a sugared biscuit by Agnes, or comforted by her when they'd scraped a knee. Now, she nodded approvingly as the siblings reached the last step. "Gud mornin', young Master and Miss," Agnes greeted them, her tone respectful but warm. She noticed a bit of lint on Alistair's sleeve and briskly dusted it off. "You're just in time. The Laird is about to lead the morning prayer."

Hand in hand, guided by Morven and trailed by Agnes, the children made their way to the dining hall. At this early hour, the long refectory table was not yet laden with the breakfast dishes, but Laird Alasdair McBeth and Lady Isobel were already standing at the head of the table along with a few assembled members of the household staff. A quiet hush fell as the family entered.

Laird Alasdair, a tall man with broad shoulders and kind, steady eyes, held a small leather-bound Bible in one hand. He gave the slightest smile as he saw his children arrive on time, and Fyonna felt a glow of pride at that approving glance. Lady Isobel stood beside her husband, elegant in a deep green morning gown, her auburn hair pinned neatly. She winked gently at Fyonna and Alistair in greeting.

Morven guided the children to stand by their parents. Agnes and two other senior servants—Finlay McQuade, the Laird's valet, and old Duncan the groundskeeper—gathered a respectful distance behind the family, heads bowed. Every morning at eight o'clock sharp, the McBeths and their household observed a brief prayer together, a tradition that infused the day with a sense of shared purpose and faith.

In a deep, clear voice that carried through the high-ceilinged hall, Laird Alasdair began to read a favourite Psalm. His Scottish brogue lent the words a musical cadence: "...Thou art my rock and my fortress; therefore for thy name's sake lead me, and guide me..." Fyonna and Alistair stood still and attentive—Alistair trying not to fidget, Fyonna with her hands folded properly in front of her—as their father's voice resonated. Lady Isobel gently placed a hand on each of their shoulders in a subtle gesture of encouragement and love.

When the reading finished, all heads bowed as Alasdair offered a short prayer for the health of his family and the well-being of those on the estate. "Amen," he concluded softly. A chorus of "Amen" echoed from those gathered, including the children. Alistair spoke the word a tad late—he had been concentrating hard on getting it right—which earned him a quietly amused glance from his mother. He ducked his head, cheeks flushed, but Lady Isobel's eyes shone with affection.

With the morning prayer concluded, the household sprang gently to action. The servants departed respectfully to their duties—Agnes to the kitchen to oversee breakfast service, Duncan back to the grounds, and Morven to accompany the children—while the McBeth family prepared to sit for breakfast.

In the dining hall, the long table was quickly dressed with steaming dishes by the efficient house staff. A footman in a neat livery placed a platter of oat porridge, still simmering, at the centre, alongside fresh-baked rolls, jars of golden honey, and a dish of butter. Another maid set out a pot of tea and warm milk for the children. The rich aromas of hearty Scottish fare—porridge, smoked kippers, and baked apples spiced with cinnamon—wafted through the air.

Fyonna and Alistair took their seats in their usual places, two chairs down from their father's seat at the head of the table. Lady Isobel sat opposite the children, her posture straight but her smile welcoming. Laird Alasdair remained standing for a moment until everyone was in place. He then nodded to Finlay, his valet, who hovered nearby ready to assist. Finlay stepped forward to pour tea for the Laird and Lady, then deftly filled the children's cups with milk. Though Finlay's primary role was attending to the Laird's personal needs, on a well-run estate everyone pitched in as needed; this morning, with the butler away on an errand, Finlay was happy to help serve the family he had known all his life.

"Thank you, Finlay," Alasdair said as the valet finished and stepped back. Only then did the Laird sit down, and the rest of the family followed—an unspoken rule that they never sat before the Laird. Despite the formality, the atmosphere at the table was gentle and familial.

"Good morning, my dears," Lady Isobel began, looking warmly at Fyonna and Alistair. "Did you sleep well?"

"Yes, Mama," Fyonna replied politely, reaching for a roll. "Morven woke us just in time. I dreamt of the loch again—" She stopped herself with a little giggle. Fyonna had an active imagination and her dreams often became breakfast table chatter.

Lady Isobel's eyes twinkled. "Ah, the loch dream. Was it the one with the swan, or something new?"

"Just the usual swan," Fyonna admitted, smiling shyly as she spread a dab of honey on her bread. "It flew over the water and I was trying to follow it."

Alasdair chuckled quietly, unfolding his napkin. "One day, Fyonna, you'll have to show me this magical dream swan of yours on our morning walk." It was well known in the family that Fyonna often slipped down to the loch's shore with her brother or Morven when allowed, drawn by the misty waters and wild swans that sometimes gathered there.

Alistair, still waking up fully, focused on spooning porridge into his bowl. Morven had stepped forward to help him, but he managed on his own, careful not to spill a drop. At twelve, he was mindful of proving himself capable of doing things without help. As he sweetened his porridge with a spoonful of brown sugar, he added, "I slept well, Father. And I remembered to wind the clock like you showed me."

"Good lad," Laird Alasdair replied, giving his son an approving nod. Alistair beamed at the recognition. One of Alasdair's small but meaningful lessons in responsibility for his son was winding the old grandfather clock in the hallway each evening—a task the boy took seriously.

Breakfast continued at an easy pace. The family ate and talked about the day ahead. Lady Isobel reminded the children of their lessons that morning. "Mrs. Fraser will be coming by at ten for your music practice," she told them, referring to their part-time piano tutor from the nearby village. Fyonna's face lit up at that—she loved piano lessons—while Alistair tried not to groan (he much preferred riding and outdoor lessons to sitting at the piano). "And before that, Morven will go over your arithmetic and writing exercises, so do your best."

"Yes, Mama," the siblings chimed in unison, though with differing levels of enthusiasm that made their parents exchange a knowing glance and smile.

In turn, Laird Alasdair outlined his own plans for the day. "I'll be riding out with Mr. Carmichael to check on the tenant farms across the river after breakfast," he said. (Mr. Carmichael was the estate's factor—the man who managed the rental accounts and dealt with the tenant farmers.) "Alistair, how would you like to accompany us? I think it's time you see how the sheep flock is faring before shearing season."

Alistair's eyes widened with excitement. He sat up straighter. "Truly, Father? I'd like that very much!" he replied eagerly, almost forgetting to address his father respectfully in his excitement. A chance to ride out with his father and observe real estate business was a treat; it made him feel grown and useful.

Alasdair hid a proud smile behind a sip of tea. "Very well. Be in the stables at nine sharp, then, in your riding boots. Finlay will help you into your riding coat after breakfast."

At this, Morven gave a tiny approving nod. She too was pleased to see Alistair taking on small duties alongside his father. "I'll see he's ready, my Laird," she assured, standing by the sideboard with her hands folded.

Lady Isobel turned her gaze to Fyonna. Not wanting her daughter to feel left out, she had something planned as well. "Fyonna, darling, I could use your help in the garden later this morning. The rose bushes by the chapel need pruning, and I think we might gather some early summer blooms to arrange for the dinner table. Would you like that?"

"Oh yes, Mother!" Fyonna answered, nearly bouncing in her seat. She loved spending time in the garden with Lady Isobel, whose flowerbeds at Clachanoch were famed for their beauty. Working side by side with her mother made her feel both grown-up and cherished.

"Good," Lady Isobel laughed softly at her daughter's obvious delight. "We'll go after your lessons then. Perhaps we'll bring a basket of flowers to old Mrs. MacLeod on our way back—her arthritis has been troubling her, and some fresh blooms might cheer her."

Fyonna nodded eagerly. She knew Mrs. MacLeod, the elderly widow of a former gamekeeper, and was glad to be included in her mother's gentle acts of kindness. The children were being quietly taught that with the privilege of their estate came the responsibility to care for those who lived on their land.

As breakfast wound down, Alasdair dabbed his mouth with his napkin and glanced at the grandfather clock through the open door—it was nearly nine. "Time to start the day in earnest," he declared. At that cue, the family rose from the table.

Alistair, remembering his opportunity, quickly handed his plate and bowl to a waiting maid to be cleared, then dashed off toward the foyer to fetch his boots—only to stop short when he caught a warning look from his mother. He hurried back and gave a polite bow to his parents. "Thank you for breakfast, Mother. Father," he said properly, a bit breathless. Fyonna mirrored him with a small curtsy.

Laird Alasdair suppressed a chuckle at his son's barely contained excitement and nodded in return. "Off you go, then. Mind Morven and Finlay's instructions," he said. With that, Alistair was truly released and he bolted away, with Morven following close behind to make sure he changed into appropriate attire for riding.

Lady Isobel took Fyonna's hand as they left the dining hall together. "We will have our own adventure soon enough, my love," she told her daughter warmly. Fyonna squeezed her mother's hand and skipped a step to keep up with her graceful stride as they headed toward the morning room to review household letters before their gardening.

Meanwhile, Laird Alasdair walked toward the front entrance hall where Finlay awaited with Alasdair's riding coat, gloves, and hat. The valet handed the coat to his master and helped him slip it on. "The bay mare is saddled and ready for you in the courtyard, sir," Finlay reported. "And young Master Alistair's pony as well. I took the liberty of having the stablehand give them both a good brushing."

"Excellent, thank you," Alasdair replied, adjusting the cuffs of his coat. Finlay then held out a neatly folded plaid wool scarf—woven in the McBeth tartan of blues and silver—should the morning wind on the moors prove brisk. Alasdair accepted it with a nod of thanks, but did not don it yet. "Not too cold today, I think," he remarked. As they walked to the door, he added in a lower voice meant just for Finlay, "How are the stables this morning? Any news?"

Finlay, ever attentive, replied with the familiarity of a long-time confidant. "All is well, sir. Rob, the stablehand, says one of the mares might foal earlier than expected, but nothing amiss. Also, the blacksmith finished the new shoes for your horse yesterday."

Alasdair gave a satisfied hum. "Very good. And Mr. Carmichael?"

"He arrived a few minutes ago, waiting for you by the stables with the ledgers, my Laird," Finlay answered as he opened the grand front door for Alasdair. Sunlight and the crisp scent of heather poured in from outside.

Standing on the front steps of the great house, Alasdair paused to inhale the fresh Highland morning. The sky was pale blue, and in the distance the rolling hills and glen of his estate were coming alive with the day. He could see Mr. Carmichael's figure by the stable, ledger under one arm. Nearby, Alistair was already mounted on his sturdy pony, doing his best to sit tall and serious in the saddle as befitting an heir accompanying his father. The sight made Alasdair's heart swell with quiet pride and amusement.

Without another word needed, Alasdair descended the steps and headed off to join his son and the factor, ready to engage in the work of running Clachanoch for the morning.

While father and son ventured out across the heather-clad hills, Lady Isobel and Fyonna began their own morning's work within the estate. First stop was the small parlour Lady Isobel used as her office. Sunlight poured into this cosy room lined with ledgers and recipe books, and a large desk held neat stacks of correspondence. Fyonna sat in a cushioned chair opposite her mother, watching intently as Lady Isobel opened the household account book.

Before Lady Isobel could begin, a polite knock sounded at the door. Agnes Sinclair stepped in, carrying a silver tray with the day's mail and a steaming pot of chamomile tea—another gentle start to the Lady's routine. "Thank you, Agnes," Lady Isobel smiled, taking the letters. "Please, have a seat for a moment. We can go over the day's menus."

Agnes perched on the edge of a chair, straight-backed and attentive. As Lady Isobel sorted through the envelopes—setting aside one to read later from her sister in Edinburgh—she addressed the housekeeper. "So, for luncheon today, I was thinking something light since the Laird and Master Alistair will likely have been riding. Perhaps the smoked trout and a barley soup?"

"That'd be fitting, me Lady," Agnes agreed promptly. "Cook has fresh cress that we canna use in thae sandwiches as well."

Fyonna watched as her mother and Agnes discussed the details of meals and household needs. She admired how smoothly her mother ran the domestic side of the estate, tending to every detail from what would be on the table to which linens would be aired for guests. Lady Isobel included her daughter by explaining each decision: why a lighter meal at midday was wise, how ensuring the servants had a hearty stew for their dinner was equally important, and even letting Fyonna seal an envelope containing a note to the baker in the village for tomorrow's bread order. These were small lessons in responsibility and leadership for the young girl, woven naturally into the morning's tasks.

After Agnes went off to oversee the kitchen with the agreed-upon plans, Lady Isobel turned to Fyonna with a smile. "Shall we tend to the roses now, darling?"

Fyonna leapt up, hardly containing her excitement. She fetched the gardening basket and gloves from the corner as Lady Isobel took up a pair of pruning shears. Thus outfitted, mother and daughter stepped out into the late-morning sun.

Outside, the gardens of Clachanoch spread out in a splendid array of colours and neat hedgerows. The estate's formal flowerbeds led toward a small stone chapel draped in ivy—one of Fyonna's favourite places. The roses along the path to the chapel were in bloom, petals unfurling in hues of pink and red.

Side by side, Lady Isobel and Fyonna knelt by the first rosebush. Lady Isobel demonstrated how to prune away a withering blossom to encourage new growth. Fyonna copied her carefully, the girl's tongue sticking out slightly in concentration as she clipped a stem with the little shears her mother had given her.

"Very good," Lady Isobel praised. She inhaled the sweet scent of a newly opened rose and added softly, "You know, your grandmother planted these very bushes when I first came to Clachanoch." Her voice held a note of fond remembrance.

"Grandmama did?" Fyonna asked in wonder. Though her maternal grandmother now lived in the Lowlands, traces of her touch were all over Clachanoch's gardens and halls.

"Yes. She wanted us to have something beautiful to look upon every morning." Lady Isobel smiled and passed a blossom to Fyonna, who cradled it as gently as a baby bird. "It's part of our family tradition to care for them, just as we care for all of Clachanoch."

They continued working in companionable peace, snipping spent blooms and gathering a basketful of vibrant flowers. Fyonna's hands grew a bit scratched despite her gloves, but she felt proud to be helping. When the basket was brimming with roses and sprigs of rosemary and heather (which Lady Isobel included for their pleasant fragrance), they stood and admired their morning's harvest.

Just then, a familiar old hound meandered up the path, sniffing at the air. It was Bran, the estate's elderly deerhound, his muzzle silvered with age. Fyonna giggled and crouched to greet him as the dog gently nosed her apron pocket, hoping for a treat. "Not now, Bran," she laughed, scratching behind his ears. "I've no biscuit for you this time."

Lady Isobel patted the dog as well. "He knows we're going visiting, I suspect," she said. "Shall we go see Mrs. MacLeod now?"

Fyonna nodded eagerly. They left their basket momentarily to wash their hands at the garden pump, then Lady Isobel retrieved a small parcel from a kitchen maid—a bundle of scones fresh from the oven, wrapped in cloth, to accompany the flowers. With Bran padding lazily behind, they walked across the yard to a pretty stone cottage at the edge of the gardens where Mrs. MacLeod lived.

The cottage door opened just as they approached, as if the occupant sensed the happy interruption. Ella MacLeod was a frail old woman, the widow of a former gamekeeper, who now lived under the McBeths' care. She broke into a toothless smile on seeing Lady Isobel and Fyonna. "My Lady! And young Miss Fyonna—what a pleasant surprise," she said in a wavering voice. She curtsied as best she could, leaning on her walking stick.

"No need for that, Mrs. MacLeod," Lady Isobel said kindly, reaching out to steady the woman. "We've come with a few things to brighten your day."

Fyonna stepped forward and presented the bouquet of roses they had gathered, now tied with a bit of twine. "These are for you, ma'am," she said, shy but pleased. "We just cut them. They smell lovely."

The old woman's eyes grew moist as she accepted the flowers, bringing them to her nose. "Och, they're bonnie indeed—thank ye, dear child."

Lady Isobel handed over the bundle of warm scones next. "And Cook insisted we deliver these to you, still warm. Be sure to have one with your tea this afternoon."

Mrs. MacLeod clasped Lady Isobel's hand in gratitude. "You're too good to me, my Lady. Both o' ye," she added, smiling at Fyonna. "The estate is blessed to have such caring folk leading it."

After a short visit—Lady Isobel made sure the old woman had everything she needed for the day and promised to send someone to fix a loose shutter on her cottage—mother and daughter took their leave. Fyonna felt a glow of happiness on the walk back. Doing these kindnesses alongside her mother showed her the importance of community and tradition at Clachanoch.

THE HEART OF THE
HIGHLANDS

By midday, Alasdair and Alistair had returned from their ride across the estate. Father and son came back invigorated and a touch mud-splattered from traversing the rolling fields. They had visited two tenant farms and the shepherd's flock on the hill, and Alistair had been brimming with questions the entire way. At one farm, he had even helped his father inspect a newborn lamb, gently holding the wobbly creature while Laird Alasdair checked its hoof. The shepherd had beamed at the young master's willingness to get his hands dirty.

When the riders trotted into the cobbled courtyard, Alistair was carrying himself with obvious pride. Alasdair clapped a hand on his son's shoulder as they dismounted, both of them laughing about how one particularly cheeky lamb had tried to nibble the Laird's hat. A stablehand hurried over to tend the horses, and father and son headed inside to clean up for lunch.

The family reconvened in the dining room for the noon meal, a bit more casually than at breakfast. Alasdair had shed his riding coat, and Alistair's cheeks were flushed from the morning's exertion as he recounted their adventures to his mother and sister.

"You should have seen Alistair with the lambs, Isobel," the Laird said, pride evident in his voice as they took their seats. "He has a gentle hand. Old Callum—the shepherd—said our boy will make a fine laird someday if he keeps that up."

Alistair tried to hide his grin in a sip of cool water. Lady Isobel reached over to squeeze his hand. "Well done, my son," she said, eyes shining.

Fyonna chimed in brightly, "I helped Mama with the roses! And we visited Mrs. MacLeod." She launched into a cheerful recounting of their visit, describing the old woman's delight at the flowers and scones.

"That's wonderful, darling," Alasdair responded. "I'm sure our roses and treats made her day. We must all take care of one another here." As servants served the light lunch of smoked trout, barley soup, and cress sandwiches, the family continued to share their morning experiences. There was an easy give-and-take across the table—parents listening with interest to their children's small triumphs, and children soaking up gentle guidance from their parents.

After lunch, the household settled into a quiet early afternoon. Laird Alasdair retreated to his study to go over some estate ledgers with Finlay's assistance. The valet-turned-secretary for the hour stood by the massive oak desk, handing his master each account book and a freshly sharpened quill. Through the study's tall windows, the sounds of the estate filtered in: distant voices of field workers, the clink of teacups as Agnes oversaw the clearing of lunch in the next room, and occasionally a burst of youthful laughter from outside where the children had been allowed a bit of playtime.

Lady Isobel, after ensuring all was in order indoors, took a moment to herself in the drawing room to read the letter from her sister. Seated on a velvet armchair near the window, she let out a soft laugh at a bit of family gossip from the Lowlands. Not far away, on the carpet, Fyonna and Alistair were playing a quiet game of chess—a recent addition to their lessons that they both took seriously. Morven sat nearby darning a small tear in one of Alistair's jackets while keeping a watchful eye (and occasionally giving a hint to Fyonna, who was less skilled at the game but determined).

By late afternoon, tea was served out on the lawn at Lady Isobel's request, since the weather was fair. Under the shade of an oak tree that had stood for a hundred years, Agnes and a maid arranged a small table with a crisp white cloth. Soon it bore a generous spread of oatcakes, berry tarts, and a teapot steaming with fragrant Earl Grey. The family gathered there for a refreshing pause.

Alasdair emerged from his study to join them, rolling his shoulders as if to shrug off work. He found Fyonna attempting to pour tea for her brother while balancing on a stool. With a chuckle, the Laird stepped in to rescue the teapot before it tipped. "Easy there, little one. I'll handle that," he said, ruffling her hair gently. Fyonna giggled and surrendered the teapot.

As they sipped tea and nibbled treats, conversation flowed lightly. They spoke of small things: a brood of ducklings spotted by the loch, the new poem Fyonna was memorising for her lessons, the way Alistair's pony liked to sneak apples from the orchard. It was in these unhurried moments that the simple grandeur of life at Clachanoch was most felt—not in ostentatious displays, but in the peace and confidence each family member had in their place and with one another.

Evening eventually cast its golden hues over the estate. The family dined together again at supper, this time in a relaxed atmosphere by the glow of oil lamps. The great oak dining table, which could host twenty in high company, now just seated the four McBeths, making it feel intimate despite the hall's lofty size. Agnes peeked in from the doorway now and then, coordinating the serving of a hearty stew made from the estate's own venison and garden vegetables. Finlay poured a dark red currant wine for the Laird and Lady, and made sure the children had their favourite raspberry cordial.

By now, the children were full of tales from the day and chattered happily between spoonfuls. Lady Isobel listened with an amused smile as Alistair tried to describe how high the sheep had jumped when startled by a fox, his arms gesturing wildly. Fyonna at one point stood on her chair to better reenact how Bran the hound had chased his tail during their tea on the lawn, which sent Alistair into peals of laughter. A gentle clearing of Alasdair's throat reminded them to mind their manners, and Fyonna sat down again with a blush and an apologetic grin. There was no anger in the Laird's quiet correction—only the steady expectation that they would remember their upbringing even in moments of excitement.

As dusk settled, the family moved to the drawing room for their customary hour of togetherness before bed. A crackling fire in the stone hearth cast dancing shadows on the walls, which were adorned with the portraits of generations of McBeth ancestors. Lady Isobel took up her embroidery hoop, gently stitching by lamplight, while Laird Alasdair selected a book of poetry from the shelf. He invited the children to sit near him on the settee. Morven hovered at the doorway, giving the family their private time but ready to escort the children to bed when the time came, and Finlay quietly set a decanter of whisky on a side table for the Laird to enjoy later.

Tonight, Alasdair decided to read aloud a few verses from Robert Burns—lines about rural life and honest labour that felt fitting after such a wholesome day. His baritone voice reciting *"My Heart's in the Highlands"* filled the room. Fyonna curled up against her mother, eyes growing heavy as she listened, while Alistair fought sleep, determined to appear grown-up enough to hear every line.

When the clock on the mantel chimed eight, Morven reappeared with a knowing smile. "Time for bed, my lambs," she said softly. Fyonna, who had been nodding off on Lady Isobel's shoulder, straightened up with a sleepy protest.

"Already?"

Lady Isobel set aside her embroidery and kissed the top of her daughter's head. "Even little roses need their rest to bloom again tomorrow," she cooed affectionately. Alistair gave a small yawn he couldn't hide. Catching his father's gentle, raised eyebrow, he conceded with a nod.

The children bid their parents goodnight with hugs—Alistair even tried to shake his father's hand in a grown-up manner before succumbing to a quick embrace, and Fyonna threw her arms around both Father and Mama. Laird Alasdair and Lady Isobel watched with contentment as Morven led the two upstairs, the nanny's arm around Fyonna while Alistair trailed a step ahead carrying a new adventure novel he planned to read before sleep.

Back in the familiar comfort of the nursery, Morven helped them change into their nightclothes. She turned down the beds and lit a small oil lamp that cast a warm golden glow in the room. The children climbed under their quilts, tiredness finally catching up with them. Alistair opened his book, but only managed a few pages before his eyelids drooped. Fyonna was already snuggled up with her doll, eyes closed as Morven gently brushed her hair one last time for the day.

Morven began to hum the same Gaelic lullaby she had that morning, the soft melody floating like a gentle breeze. In a half-whisper, she sang an old blessing in Scots Gaelic over them, words that had soothed McBeth children for generations. Neither child understood every word of the ancient tongue, but the meaning was clear in Morven's tender tone. It spoke of protection through the night and joy in the morning.

Lady Isobel and Laird Alasdair stepped quietly into the nursery just as Morven finished her song, having come to kiss their children goodnight as they did every evening. Isobel moved first to Fyonna's bed, seeing her daughter already mostly asleep, and pulled the blanket up to her chin. Fyonna's eyes fluttered open briefly. "Goodnight, Mama," she murmured. "Goodnight, my darling girl," Lady Isobel whispered, kissing her brow.

Alasdair stood by Alistair's bed. The boy was valiantly trying to appear awake, the open book still propped on his chest. Alasdair chuckled under his breath and gently took the book from his son's hands. "You can finish the tale tomorrow, son," he said quietly. Alistair nodded, finally relenting to fatigue. "Thank you for today, Father," he managed to say, a smile of pure contentment on his face. The Laird placed a firm, loving hand on Alistair's shoulder. "Sleep well, my boy. I'm proud of you," he replied softly, ruffling the lad's hair one last time.

With final hugs and whispered blessings, the parents and Morven left the children to their dreams.

Outside the nursery door, Lady Isobel looped her arm through her husband's as they walked down the dim corridor toward their own chambers. A single harp-like note plucked by the wind echoed from somewhere in the hills outside, and the night settled over Clachanoch Estate.

In the cosy darkness of the nursery, Fyonna and Alistair drifted to sleep feeling safe, loved, and ready for whatever adventures the next day at Clachanoch would bring. Their home was not just a grand estate of stone walls and vast lands—it was a living tapestry of family, faithful staff, and cherished traditions. The routines might be structured and the halls steeped in age-old customs, but warmth and love filled every corner. Life at Clachanoch Estate moved with the sun and seasons in an easy rhythm, each day much like this one: full of gentle duty, kindness, and the simple, enduring grandeur of family life in the Highland way.

FORTUNE IN STONE

The Highland winds whispered secrets through the ancient stones of Clachanoch Estate, carrying the scent of heather and peat across the vast lands that had been home to the McBeths for generations. Laird Alasdair McBeth stood atop the ridge, gazing over his domain. Though Clachanoch thrived under his stewardship, an unease stirred within him—a sense of urgency he could not quite name. The land was bountiful now, but fortune could be fickle. It was his duty to ensure his family's security, not just for the present, but for the uncertain days ahead.

One evening, as the last light of the sun dipped below the hills, Alasdair retreated to his study. He unrolled a map of the estate, his fingers tracing the contours of the land he knew so well. His mind turned to the wealth Clachanoch had amassed over the years—gold, silver, and precious goods gathered from trade and careful dealings. Wealth was a blessing, but it could also be a curse. He had seen estates fall when fortune turned, families left with nothing but memories of past glories. He would not let that happen to his own.

Determined, Alasdair set about a clandestine plan. Late that night, when all was still, he moved through the halls of Clachanoch with purpose. He climbed the turret stairs, the stone steps cold beneath his boots, until he reached the highest chamber. There, hidden in a recess long forgotten by all but the laird himself, he secured a portion of the family's wealth—gold bars that gleamed dully in the moonlight. It was not mere hoarding; it was protection, a shield against future calamity.

Yet, he was not finished. In the days that followed, Alasdair sought another hiding place, one closer to the heart of the estate. Beneath the great hearth in the kitchen, concealed behind a loose stone, lay a second cache of bullion. Only his most trusted men knew of its existence, and even then, the full extent of his preparations remained a secret known only to himself. His will contained vague references, instructions to be followed only if dire need arose. The McBeth legacy would not be squandered.

While Alasdair worked in secrecy, the estate itself remained a hub of Highland life, flourishing under the steady hands of those who lived and worked within its walls. Lady Isobel, ever the pillar of grace, managed the household with quiet efficiency. The servants carried out their duties with diligence, ensuring the estate functioned like a well-tended machine.

"A grand sight, is it not?" Isobel murmured one morning as she and Alasdair stood on the manor's balcony, watching the estate come to life.

"Aye," Alasdair replied, a touch of wistfulness in his tone. "But prosperity can turn faster than a Highland storm. We must be ready for whatever comes."

Isobel turned to study her husband, sensing the weight of responsibility pressing upon him. "Clachanoch has endured because of those who came before us, and it will endure because of those who follow. But ye cannot carry the burden alone."

Alasdair gave a small nod, though he did not speak further of his concerns. Instead, he let his gaze drift to their children, Alistair and Fyonna, playing in the courtyard below. They were still young, but one day they would be the stewards of this land. It was for them that he took these precautions, for them that he safeguarded their inheritance.

As the sun set on Clachanoch, the estate bustled with preparations for the evening feast. The aroma of roasting meats and freshly baked bread filled the halls, mingling with the sound of laughter and Highland melodies. The harvest had been plentiful, and tonight, the McBeths would celebrate.

In the great hall, servants moved swiftly, placing platters of food on the long dining table. Donald Fraser, the estate's cook, presided over the kitchen with his usual mix of gruffness and pride, ensuring every dish was perfect.

"Donald, the pheasant smells divine," Agnes Sinclair observed as she inspected the preparations.

"Aye, it's comin' along nicely," Donald replied, nodding in satisfaction. "We'll give the laird a feast worth rememberin'."

As twilight deepened, the guests arrived, filling the hall with warmth and revelry. Music played, led by a fiddler whose lively tune set feet tapping and hands clapping. Laird Alasdair and Lady Isobel stood at the head of the table, toasting to the land, the people, and the legacy they all shared.

"To Clachanoch," Alasdair declared, his voice strong. "May she stand as a beacon of strength and prosperity for generations to come."

"Here, here!" came the resounding response, followed by the clinking of glasses and the hum of conversation.

Among the guests were neighbouring lairds, cousins from the Lowlands, and trusted allies from the village, all of whom had gathered not only to enjoy the feast but to show respect for the McBeths' stewardship. Isobel moved among them with graceful ease, offering warm words and thoughtful glances, while Alasdair listened intently to every tale of land and kin, his hand never straying far from his wife's.

As the evening wore on, Alistair and Fyonna joined the ceilidh, laughing and dancing among the guests. Isobel smiled, watching her children revel in the joy of the moment.

Later that night, when the music had faded and the guests had departed, Alasdair and Isobel lingered a while longer in the great hall. He took her hand and drew her close, the flickering candlelight casting golden shadows across her face. "Without ye, this would all be stone and duty," he whispered. "Ye are the soul of Clachanoch, Isobel." She rested her head on his chest, his heartbeat steady beneath her ear. "And you, my love, are its strength."

Alasdair, however, found his thoughts returning to the wealth hidden within Clachanoch's walls. His mind did not linger on gold for its own sake, but on what it represented—security, resilience, the ability to weather any storm. He had done what he could to protect his family's future. The rest, as always, would be in the hands of fate.

As the fire burned low and the last of the guests took their leave, Alasdair and Isobel sat together in the quiet of their chambers. The estate thrived, their children flourished, and the Highlands stretched endlessly beyond their windows, steadfast and enduring. For now, all was well. And yet, Alasdair knew better than most that peace was never eternal.

"Ye've done well, Alasdair," Isobel said softly, resting a hand on his. "The estate is strong, and so is our family."

He met her gaze, nodding. "Aye. But strength must be safeguarded, Isobel. Always."

He reached across to take both her hands in his. "If anything were to happen tae me... I want ye to ken I've put things in place. For the bairns. For you." Isobel's eyes glistened but she held his gaze with unflinching resolve. "Then I'll trust in what ye've done, Alasdair. And I'll carry it forward, as we've always done—together."

Outside their window, the moon cast silver light over the moors, and somewhere in the distance, a lone owl called into the night. The world was still, if only for a moment, and Clachanoch stood strong in that silence, a sanctuary built not just of stone, but of love, legacy, and the quiet courage of those who called it home.

The Highland winds howled across the moors, carrying whispers of times past and times yet to come. Clachanoch stood firm, as it always had—but whether it would weather the storms ahead remained to be seen.

HIGHLAND RESURGENCE

The flickering candlelight cast dancing shadows on the walls of Laird Alasdair McBeth's study as he awaited the arrival of the local farmers. Spread before him was a detailed map of Clachanoch Estate, its worn edges a testament to the years of stewardship and care it had endured. The economy was starting to falter, and whispers of change were beginning to reach their small corner of the world. Alasdair knew that he needed the support of his neighbours now more than ever.

The farmers arrived in twos and threes, stamping the cold from their boots as they entered the study. Each was greeted warmly by Alasdair, who offered them a dram of whisky before they settled around the great oak table. The fire crackled in the hearth, but there was no mistaking the unease in the air.

Lachlan MacKenzie, with his weathered face and calloused hands, was the first to speak. "Laird McBeth, times are changin'. The economy's falterin', and there's more talk o' reform than I've ever heard before. We cannae ignore it."

Mairi MacDonald nodded, her hands clasped in front of her. "Aye, Sir, Lachlan's right. We cannae rely on the estate alone tae keep us goin'. We need tae find ways tae sustain ourselves, no matter what happens."

Jamie MacIntyre, the youngest among them, leaned forward, his eyes bright with determination. "We need tae modernise, Sir. There's new techniques bein' used elsewhere—crop rotation, different livestock breeds, better tools. If we embrace some o' these changes, we'll be better prepared."

Eilidh Stewart, her expression firm, added, "But we cannae forget our roots. Our way o' life is worth preservin', aye? There's ways tae adapt while still honourin' the land as our ancestors did."

Alasdair listened intently, his hands clasped before him as he considered their words. Finally, he spoke, his voice calm but firm. "You're all right. We must act now to safeguard our future. This land has provided for us for generations, but we cannot afford to be complacent. If we stand together, we will weather this storm."

Lady Isobel stood just beyond the study door, quietly observing the gathering from the corridor. She had seen the burden in her husband's eyes and knew how deeply he cared for those who looked to him for leadership. She stepped into the room, offering a gentle smile as she crossed to Alasdair's side, placing a steadying hand on his arm. Her presence alone reminded the gathered farmers that strength came not only from the Laird but from the Lady beside him.

The murmurs of agreement settled into serious discussion. The men and women leaned over the map as ideas took shape—better irrigation, new crops, livestock improvements, and shared resources. They discussed setting up a marketplace where farmers could trade surplus goods and ensure that the whole community thrived, not just the estate.

As the meeting drew to a close, Alasdair stood and clasped each farmer's hand in turn. "We may face uncertain times, but as long as we stand together, we can overcome any obstacle."

The following weeks saw an immense effort take hold of Clachanoch. The fields, once battered by harsh winters, were ploughed and prepped with renewed vigour. Lachlan MacKenzie led the charge in improving irrigation, ensuring every drop of water was put to good use. Mairi MacDonald shared her knowledge of herbal remedies, helping keep both people and livestock healthy. Jamie MacIntyre tested new farming techniques, and Eilidh Stewart organised bartering markets to ensure that every family had enough to get by.

The estate's smithy became a central hub of activity. Children delivered baskets of bread to neighbours while the older folk shared tales around the fire, laughter blending with the rhythmic clang of hammer on iron. Lady Isobel organised sewing circles and teaching days, offering not only clothing but knowledge—preserving the old ways while helping the next generation prepare for new challenges.

One evening, as Alasdair sat by the hearth reflecting on the progress made, a knock came at the door. It was the local blacksmith, Torin McLeen, who had heard of the Laird's efforts and wanted to offer his services.

"Ye've inspired us all, Sir," Torin said, shifting his weight awkwardly. "We're all in this together, an' we'll support ye however we can."

Alasdair clasped the man's shoulder. "Your help is most welcome, Torin. A strong community is only as good as those who work together."

The next day, Torin set to work repairing farming tools, reinforcing wooden carts, and ensuring the estate's blacksmithing needs were met. Soon after, a travelling engineer, Brodie MacLaren, arrived, offering new ideas on estate improvements. With his guidance, the estate introduced wind-powered irrigation and made efficiency improvements to farming practices.

As new friendships formed and distant kin returned to lend their hands, the McBeths welcomed them with open arms. The great hall of Clachanoch was once more filled with song and stories by firelight. What had started as a meeting among farmers had grown into a movement—a Highland resurgence.

The changes did not go unnoticed. Neighbouring estates began to take interest in Clachanoch's success, and soon Laird Seth Bryden arrived to discuss a partnership between their lands.

"Sir Alasdair, we both stand to gain from workin' together," Seth said as they walked the fields. "Our combined resources could do wonders for this part o' the Highlands."

Alasdair nodded thoughtfully. "Aye, Seth, I believe we could accomplish a great deal. Unity will always be our greatest strength."

Over the next year, Clachanoch grew in both prosperity and renown. The once-faltering economy had stabilised, thanks in large part to the combined efforts of the estate's people and its allies. The windmill stood as a symbol of progress, the new markets thrived, and the land itself seemed to hum with renewed life.

On the eve of the midsummer festival, the estate lit lanterns from one end to the other. Families gathered with baskets of food and bottles of elderflower wine. Musicians played beneath the ancient oak, and for one glorious night, the moors echoed with laughter and hope.

One evening, as Alasdair stood with Isobel on the manor's veranda, watching the sun set over their lands, he exhaled slowly.

"We've faced challenges before," he murmured, taking in the sight of his people, their laughter ringing through the courtyard below. "But this time... I think we've truly set a course for something greater."

Isobel smiled, slipping her arm through his. "You've done more than secure our future, Alasdair. You've given our people hope."

He turned to face her fully then, cupping her cheek in his rough hand. "And I've never done it alone," he said gently. "It's you, Isobel. You've stood beside me through every trial." She leaned into his touch, their foreheads resting together, the sunset casting its final golden rays across their joined silhouettes.

As the stars emerged, Clachanoch stood strong, its foundations not just of stone, but of unity, resilience, and the unyielding Highland spirit.

SHADOWS OVER CLACHANOCH

The Clachanoch Estate stood as a testament to Laird Alasdair McBeth's unwavering dedication. Under his stewardship, the land flourished, the community thrived, and the estate became a beacon of stability in an ever-changing world. Yet even the strongest walls could not keep illness at bay.

For weeks, Alasdair had fought against a fever that came and went like the Highland mist, leaving him weak and breathless. At first, he brushed it off as a passing ailment, refusing to be confined to his chambers. But as his strength waned and his once-commanding stride faltered, Lady Isobel grew increasingly concerned. The finest physicians were summoned, their remedies ranging from herbal tinctures to the latest medical treatments, but nothing could halt the affliction tightening its grip on him.

The household staff moved in hushed tones, their concern evident in their solemn expressions. The air within the grand manor grew thick with unease, an unspoken understanding settling over Clachanoch: their Laird was slipping away.

One evening, as a storm howled outside, rattling the windows and shaking the old stone walls, Alasdair beckoned his wife and children to his bedside. The flickering candlelight cast long shadows across the room, dancing in rhythm with the wavering breath of the man they loved.

"Isobel," he murmured, his voice rough but steady. "You must promise me—Clachanoch must stand. It is more than land, more than a title. It is our heart."

Lady Isobel grasped his hand, her own trembling. "I swear it, Alasdair. We will honour everything you built."

He turned his weary gaze to Alastair, his eldest. "Son, ye are ready. This land—this people—will look to you now. Lead them well."

Alastair swallowed against the lump in his throat and nodded. "Yes, Father. I will do right by you."

Finally, his eyes found Fyonna, the fire of his lineage burning bright in her sorrowful gaze. "And ye, my lass, you will do great things. Never let the world tell you otherwise."

With a final exhale, Laird Alasdair McBeth, the man who had shaped Clachanoch into a sanctuary of strength and prosperity, fell into eternal sleep.

The day of the funeral dawned grey and unrelenting, the sky weeping in quiet lamentation. The McBeth family stood at the grave, the weight of loss pressing upon them like the heavy Highland clouds. Friends and neighbours had come from far and wide to pay their respects, their voices low as they murmured prayers in Gaelic, a language as old as the land itself.

Lady Isobel stood between her children, her black mourning dress rippling slightly in the cold wind. Though grief threatened to consume her, she remained composed, a pillar of quiet dignity. Alastair, now the new Laird of Clachanoch, kept his shoulders squared, though his hands clenched into fists at his sides. Fyonna's tears ran freely, her hand tightly gripping her mother's.

Trembling with emotion as he spoke of Alasdair's strength, compassion, and unwavering sense of duty, the minister carried on. His words painted a portrait of a man not only revered by his peers but deeply loved by his people. Even those who had once disagreed with Alasdair's choices now wept openly, recognising the loss of a man whose life had been devoted to others.

As the minister's voice carried over the mourners, whispering of life beyond, a sudden hush fell over the gathering. A shift in the wind, a rustling beyond the trees—something unseen yet deeply felt. The mourners shivered as if an unseen presence watched from the shadows of the moors.

Some said later that they felt Alasdair's spirit pass through them like a warm breeze—just for a moment. An unseen hand on the shoulder. A whisper of thanks. It was fleeting, but it comforted many, including Lady Isobel, who closed her eyes and smiled softly through her tears.

The service concluded, and the community stepped forward to offer their condolences. Lachlan MacKenzie, his weathered face lined with sorrow, was among the first. "Ye ken we stand wi' ye, Laird Alastair. Whatever ye need, Clachanoch will no' be left wantin'."

"Thank you, Lachlan," Alastair replied, his voice steady despite the turmoil within him.

Mairi MacDonald clasped Lady Isobel's hands. "He was a good man, ma'am. A great man."

Lady Isobel gave a small nod, unable to trust her voice.

As evening fell over the estate, the halls of Clachanoch felt emptier than before. Friends and neighbours departed, leaving the family to grieve in silence. Alastair retreated to his father's study, staring at the stacks of ledgers and maps that now belonged to him. Fyonna wandered the halls, pausing at windows to watch the landscape her father had cherished.

Lady Isobel sat alone in the drawing room, the firelight flickering against her weary face. The estate still stood, but something in the air had shifted. An unspoken warning lingered in the silence, a presence just beyond reach.

In the nursery, Fyonna found one of her father's tartan scarves draped over the back of a chair. She pulled it to her chest and breathed in his scent, allowing the tears to fall freely now that no one was watching. Alistair found her there not long after and simply sat beside her, their silence speaking more than words ever could.

Upstairs, Isobel finally entered their chamber alone for the first time. She touched the pillow where her husband had lain and whispered a private goodbye. Then, squaring her shoulders, she turned toward the window where the stars were beginning to appear over the moors. She would hold this place together—for her children, for the people, and for the man who had entrusted it all to her care.

And somewhere in the darkness beyond the manor, hidden from sight, something watched.

THE SERPENT IN SILK

The air in Clachanoch was heavy with change, though no one could quite name its source. The land, once steady beneath their feet, now seemed to shift with an unsettling energy. The wind carried whispers through the halls of the grand manor, and in its wake, something unseen stirred. And yet, amid these quiet undercurrents, a new presence had arrived—one that would weave herself into the very fabric of their lives with an elegance as beguiling as it was dangerous.

Vera Blackbourne was unlike any woman Clachanoch had seen before. With dark auburn hair that shimmered like burnished copper in the candlelight and eyes that held the promise of secrets, she moved through the estate as though she had always belonged there. Draped in silk and lace, with perfume that lingered in rooms long after she had left them, she was a creature of refinement and charm, and she knew how to wield them both to great effect.

Her arrival had been met with hushed curiosity. She came from the Lowlands, or so she claimed, but her accent bore the faintest traces of foreign lands. She was well-versed in art and music, well-read in matters of politics and society, and her manner suggested a familiarity with privilege. It was no surprise that she caught Alastair McBeth's eye.

Lady Isobel watched with growing unease as her son was drawn ever deeper into Vera's world. Though outwardly gracious, she saw through the veneer of practised charm. Vera had an undeniable magnetism, but there was something too polished about her words, too rehearsed in her affections. Isobel had spent a lifetime reading people, and Vera Blackbourne was not what she seemed.

Behind closed doors, Vera had already begun making suggestions—innocent enough at first. New curtains for the drawing room, a different cut of dress for Fyonna, a little more modern décor in the study. Then came bolder remarks: dismissing long-serving staff for being 'behind the times', questioning Agnes Sinclair's authority, or insisting certain guests be uninvited because they didn't fit 'the new vision for Clachanoch'.

Fyonna, too, sensed something amiss. Unlike her mother, she did not mask her suspicions. "She's a snake, Alastair," she muttered one evening as they stood on the terrace, overlooking the moonlit hills.

Alastair sighed, running a hand through his hair. "You've never given her a chance, Fyonna. She's not as you think. She has vision, ambition—"

"She has you," Fyonna cut in sharply. "And that's what she wants most of all."

At dinner, Vera took to rearranging the seating plans, subtly removing Isobel from her place of honour beside her son. Fyonna found herself silenced by passive-aggressive compliments: "Oh, you're quite the fiery little thing, aren't you?" Vera would purr with a smile so sweet it curdled the soup. The servants, long loyal to the McBeths, began to refer to her behind her back as 'the silk serpent'.

Alastair shook his head, unwilling to entertain the thought. Vera was unlike anyone he had ever known, and she made him feel something he could not explain. There was excitement in her company, a sense of stepping into a world larger than the one he had always known. She spoke of progress, of wealth beyond the fields and pastures, of Clachanoch as more than a mere Highland estate but a beacon of modernity and prestige.

What Alastair failed to see was the slow unravelling of the estate's harmony in Vera's wake. The servants whispered of her imperious nature, of the way she looked down upon their traditions with thinly veiled disdain. The villagers, once so welcomed within Clachanoch's walls, now found the doors closed more often than not. She was reshaping Alastair's world, thread by delicate thread, until soon, there would be nothing left of the life he had once known.

Lady Isobel's suspicions deepened when she found Vera attempting to charm the estate solicitor. Their voices were low in the drawing room, Vera leaning in close, her hand resting ever so casually on the man's forearm. When Isobel entered, Vera merely smiled and said, "We were discussing future prospects." It took all of Isobel's restraint not to throw the woman out then and there.

One evening, Lady Isobel found Vera standing before the great portrait of Laird Alasdair McBeth, her gaze contemplative.

"You never met him," Isobel said quietly, stepping into the room. "But you study him as though you did."

Vera turned with a slow smile. "He built something great," she murmured. "It would be a shame to see it squandered."

Isobel's expression did not waver. "And you believe you can preserve it?"

"Oh, my lady, I do not believe—I know." Vera's fingers trailed along the gilded frame of the portrait before she met Isobel's gaze. "Alastair has a mind for greatness, but he needs guidance. He needs someone who sees what Clachanoch could be, not just what it was."

"Alastair needs his family," Isobel countered, her voice firm.

"Of course," Vera said smoothly. "But one mustn't let sentiment cloud progress."

As she turned to leave, she caught sight of her reflection in the glass of the drawing room cabinet and paused, adjusting a loose curl. "Sentiment," she said softly, as if tasting the word. "It's a beautiful thing, in small doses." Then she glided away, leaving the scent of roses and something bitter in her wake.

As she left the room, her skirts whispering against the stone floor, Isobel felt a chill creep up her spine. She knew now, beyond doubt—Vera Blackbourne was not simply here for Alastair's heart. She was here for all of Clachanoch.

And she would not stop until it was hers.

WINDS OF CHANGE

The great halls of Clachanoch Estate, once brimming with warmth and laughter, now stood as hollow echoes of their former glory. Where once the household had thrived under the careful stewardship of Laird Alasdair McBeth, now it faltered under the weight of extravagance and unchecked ambition. The cause? A woman with a hunger insatiable—Lady Vera McBeth.

Alastair had married Vera in a ceremony befitting the prestige of Clachanoch. The grand halls had been filled with guests, the finest musicians had played reels into the night, and no expense had been spared on the wedding feast. It had been a spectacle, a declaration of Vera's arrival as the new Lady of Clachanoch. But beneath the gilded façade, something far darker lurked. For Vera's love of splendour did not end with her wedding day—it only intensified.

She spent money as if it were endless, demanding new gowns, jewellery, imported wines, and furnishings fit for the highest of nobility. Lavish parties became a regular occurrence, and the estate's wealth dwindled under the strain of Vera's insatiable desires. The more Alastair pleaded for caution, the more she mocked him.

"You are a McBeth, Alastair," she scoffed one evening, draped in silks from France. "Do you think our ancestors built this estate by pinching pennies? Clachanoch must exude power, or it will fall into ruin."

Alastair gritted his teeth. "Vera, you are driving it into ruin! There is no more money to squander. The crops did poorly last season, trade routes are shifting, and our coffers are nearly empty."

She waved a dismissive hand, sipping her wine. "Then find more money. You're the Laird, aren't you?"

And so, to appease his wife and keep the estate afloat, Alastair sold off parcels of land—woodlands, grazing pastures, even treasured family heirlooms. The staff murmured, the community whispered, and still, Vera spent.

Even the children of the village, once free to roam Clachanoch's orchards and fish in the loch, found themselves turned away at the gates. Vera called them urchins. She didn't like their smudged cheeks or their curious eyes. She had the iron fence reinforced and posted a guard. When Lady Isobel objected, Vera laughed coldly and said,

"A grand estate must have boundaries. We're not running a charity, after all."

Lady Isobel, ever the steady hand of Clachanoch, watched her son struggle under the weight of his wife's excesses. She saw the pain in his eyes, the lines of stress deepening upon his brow. Though grief for Alasdair still sat heavy in her heart, she had carried on—for the estate, for her children, for the legacy she had helped build.

But Clachanoch was changing, and not for the better.

At one of Vera's so-called soirées, she paraded through the drawing room in a sapphire gown stitched with seed pearls, claiming it had belonged to a countess in Vienna. She made Lady Isobel sit at the far end of the table and introduced her to guests as "Alastair's dear, old mother," her voice honeyed with poison. Fyonna stormed out that evening, unable to bear another insult thinly veiled in charm.

Servants, unpaid for months, began to leave. Farmers could not afford to remain on the land. The estate, once a beacon of prosperity, now whispered of failure.

Lady Isobel's heart—already burdened by grief—could not bear it.

One bitterly cold morning, she collapsed while walking the halls of the manor. Fyonna, who had been at her side, cried out in terror as she caught her mother's frail body before it struck the stone floor. She called for help, but the household had grown quiet—so many had left, and those who remained hesitated, fearing Vera's wrath.

Alastair came running, falling to his knees beside his mother.

"Mother, stay with me," he pleaded, his hands trembling as he held hers. "We'll get the doctor. You'll be all right."

Lady Isobel, ever graceful even in suffering, offered her son a weak smile. "No, my boy. My heart has carried too much. It was never meant to hold so much sorrow."

Tears filled Alastair's eyes. "Please, don't leave us."

With a final breath, she squeezed his hand. "Be wise, Alastair... Be strong."

Then, the light faded from her eyes.

Fyonna let out a wail that could have shattered the very stones of Clachanoch. The estate had lost its heart. And Vera?

She was in the parlour, reclining with a book of French verse, sipping wine before a blazing fire. When the news was delivered, she pursed her lips and remarked, "Well, at least the mourning wardrobe I had made will now serve its purpose."

She merely looked upon the scene with an impassive gaze and turned away.

The day of Lady Isobel's funeral was marked by howling winds and bitter cold. The people of the estate, the villagers who had once flourished under the McBeths, gathered to pay their respects. They had loved her—she had been kind and just, a woman who understood the land and those who worked it.

Vera arrived at the service fashionably late, clad in a gown of deepest black velvet with a hat so wide it blocked the view of three mourners behind her. She did not shed a tear. Instead, she whispered to a guest beside her, "Let them weep. I have other matters to tend to." It was Fyonna who heard her—and Fyonna who clenched her jaw until it ached.

Alastair stood at the graveside, his shoulders slumped under the weight of his failure. He had failed his father's legacy, failed the estate, failed his mother. Clachanoch was no longer a stronghold; it was a plundered relic, stripped of its grandeur, its spirit broken under the tyranny of his wife.

That evening, he sat alone in his father's study, the very place where Alasdair had governed Clachanoch with steady hands and clear eyes. The fire burned low, the ledgers before him painting a picture of ruin.

He exhaled a ragged breath and lifted his gaze to the grand portrait of his father.

"I've destroyed it, Father," he whispered into the empty room. "I let her take everything. The land, the people, the dignity of this place." His hands clenched into fists. "I was supposed to be strong. I was supposed to protect it."

A noise at the door startled him. He turned to find Fyonna standing there, grief-stricken but determined. "We can't save it, Alastair. We have to leave."

His stomach twisted. He knew she was right. The debts were insurmountable, the trust of the people broken, the estate crumbling under the weight of decay. Clachanoch was dying, and nothing—not even the strongest of McBeth wills—could resurrect it now.

For the first time in months, he allowed himself to feel the full ache of regret—not just for the land, but for the people he had driven away. For the joy that had once filled these halls. For the father whose legacy now lay buried with the mother who had tried to hold it all together.

As the last embers in the hearth flickered and dimmed, so too did Alastair's hope. Clachanoch, the great estate of his ancestors, was lost.

And Vera McBeth, the woman he had once believed he loved, had been its ruin.

The day they left Clachanoch, the sky was overcast, heavy with unfallen rain. Alastair stood at the doorway, looking back one final time at the home that had been his life, his burden, his greatest shame.

Vera was nowhere to be seen—likely wrapped in her silks, lamenting the loss of her status more than the estate itself. Fyonna stood beside her brother, her hands tightening into fists.

"She never loved this place, Alastair. She only loved what it could give her."

Alastair swallowed hard and gave a final nod. "Aye. But it doesn't matter now. It's over."

The great doors of Clachanoch closed behind them, and the estate, once a beacon of Highland pride, fell into silence.

The era of the McBeths at Clachanoch had come to an end.

THE DISPERSAL

As the final rays of sunlight faded from the sky, casting a sombre glow over Clachanoch Estate, Alastair Mc-Beth stood before the imposing gates, his shoulders heavy with the weight of failure. The once-grand manor behind him loomed in silence, its windows dark, its halls empty. The great house that had once echoed with laughter and purpose now felt like a tomb—one he had helped seal shut.

Fyonna, by his side, stared at the weathered stones of their ancestral home, her expression unreadable. The estate had suffered irreparably under the excesses of Vera, who had bled their resources dry and ensured that any hope of salvaging Clachanoch was crushed beneath an avalanche of debts. The secret provision in their father's will—his last safeguard for Clachanoch—had been their final hope. Yet, when the lawyers came with their ledgers and stern expressions, they revealed the brutal truth. The clause could only be activated if Alastair had proved himself a responsible steward of the estate. Instead, Vera's indulgence and his failure to rein her in had sealed their doom. Had Vera known of this hidden wealth, would she have curbed her spending? Alastair doubted it. The greed in her was too deeply rooted, her thirst for status too unquenchable.

The meeting with the lawyers had been swift and decisive. The ledgers told a clear story of excess, of coin spent frivolously while the estate withered. Clachanoch had been bled dry, and the hidden provision—gold and silver bars tucked away in secret—was now lost to them. The lawyers had left with their final verdict, leaving Alastair to drown in his own remorse.

"I should have known," he muttered under his breath, gripping the wrought-iron gate so tightly his knuckles turned white. "I should have fought harder."

Fyonna turned to him, her eyes filled with something between sorrow and disappointment. "Aye, ye should have," she said softly. "But regret changes nought. We can't save Clachanoch. We can only choose how we leave it."

With a final glance at their childhood home, they turned away, leaving behind the only place they had ever known.

Alastair and Vera relocated to the town, clinging to what little they had left. A townhouse—grand in comparison to the homes around it, but a shadow of the estate they had lost—became their new residence. They kept only a few staff, for even Vera could no longer afford extravagance. But even in reduced circumstances, her spending did not cease entirely. If there was money to be spent, she would find a way to spend it.

The townhouse sat at the end of a narrow cobbled lane, respectable on the outside, but filled with tension within. Neighbours noticed the strained silences between husband and wife, the way Vera's laughter had lost its sparkle, and how Alastair's once-confident stride had become a weary shuffle. The drawing room curtains stayed closed more often than not, and the parties Vera once thrived on became fewer, quieter, lonelier.

It was here, in the confines of the townhouse, that their marriage, already crumbling, finally shattered.

One evening, after another argument over finances, Alastair snapped. "You never knew when enough was enough! You wasted every coin we had, and now look at us! Clachanoch is gone, and it's your doing!"

Vera's eyes flashed with fury. "Don't you dare blame me for your failures, Alastair! You were weak! You let it happen! You let me do as I pleased, and now you want to weep over the ruins? Pitiful!"

Alastair felt his breath hitch, pain stabbing at his chest. His vision swam. He stumbled back, clutching at his heart, his breathing turning ragged.

Vera's rage faltered. "Alastair?"

He couldn't answer. A sharp, searing pain gripped his chest, and his legs buckled beneath him. The last thing he saw was Vera, eyes wide in horror, reaching for him as he collapsed.

Alastair awoke in a hospital bed, his body weak, his mind slow. A doctor stood at his side, explaining in calm, clinical tones that he had suffered a heart attack—likely brought on by stress.

Vera was nowhere to be seen.

He felt no relief, only a hollow emptiness.

When she did come, days later, her face was drawn, her voice softer than he had ever heard it. "Alastair... I was wrong."

He stared at her, exhaustion making his voice hoarse. "Too late, Vera."

Tears welled in her eyes. "I'll change. I'll do better. We can start again."

He closed his eyes. "No, we can't."

And so, without ceremony, Vera left. No one knew where she went, nor did they care to find out.

In her absence, Alastair began the slow work of survival—not redemption, for he believed himself beyond that—but simply existing. He took on modest work advising a legal firm on land use, using the remnants of his once-great education and experience. His name still held enough weight to open doors, though fewer than before. In the quiet moments, he would look out over the rooftops and wonder if the winds from Clachanoch ever reached this far.

Fyonna returned one last time to Clachanoch, though she already knew the truth—there was nothing left to salvage. She walked through the empty halls, running her fingers along dust-covered furniture, gazing at the portraits of their ancestors with regret. The house, still as grand as ever in structure, felt lifeless.

She had considered selling the furniture, but she couldn't bring herself to do it. It wasn't just wood and fabric. It was history.

In the nursery, she found a small wooden toy Alistair had carved for her when they were children—a stag, its antlers chipped but noble. She cradled it in her hands and sat on the old window seat, staring out at the moors. A storm was rolling in, the clouds thick and low. The house, too, seemed to brace for it, as if mourning its own decline.

Instead, she covered everything with white sheets, drawing the curtains and shutters closed, sealing the house in quiet darkness.

Alastair did not come. She did not ask him to.

As she locked the doors for the final time, a gust of wind stirred through the trees, rustling the ivy that had begun creeping up the stone walls. The estate would stand as it always had, waiting in silence, its halls empty, its past lingering in whispers through the corridors.

Before she turned away, Fyonna pressed her hand to the great front door. "You were home," she whispered. "And maybe... one day... you will be again." Her breath caught in her throat, and for a moment, she thought she heard a faint echo of children's laughter, as though the walls themselves remembered.

Perhaps, one day, someone would return.

But for now, Clachanoch slept.

And with that, Fyonna walked away, leaving the past behind, stepping into whatever future awaited her.

A LEGACY BEYOND TIME

Years passed, and life carried on in its ever-changing rhythm. Fyonna found solace in the path she had chosen, building a life rooted in purpose and love. She became a respected teacher, guiding generations of children and passing down not only knowledge but also the wisdom of her forebears. She married a kind-hearted man who shared her love for education and community, and together, they raised a family filled with warmth and laughter. The past remained a treasured part of her story, but she did not allow it to define her future.

Alistair, too, found a quieter form of peace. Though Clachanoch had slipped through his grasp, he had reclaimed something more valuable—a sense of self beyond titles and land. He lived simply in a modest home, tending to his small garden with hands that once bore the weight of a Laird's burdens. The town accepted him for who he was, not what he had lost, and he became a source of quiet wisdom for those who sought his advice. He would often be found speaking with the local children, sharing tales of resilience and the importance of honouring one's roots while forging one's own path.

One spring afternoon, Fyonna sat in her garden, surrounded by her grandchildren. The scent of lavender and roses lingered in the air as the children nestled around her, eager for another tale of the past.

"Grandmother, tell us about Clachanoch," one of the little ones asked, wide-eyed with curiosity.

Fyonna smiled, brushing a hand over the curls of her youngest granddaughter. "Clachanoch was more than just a grand house or a vast estate," she began, her voice gentle. "It was the heart of our family, a place where the land and its people were bound together by history, hardship, and hope."

She told them of the sprawling gardens, the proud halls, and the gatherings where music and laughter filled the air. She spoke of her father, Laird Alasdair McBeth, and the strength he carried, the sacrifices he made. The children hung on her every word, their imaginations painting pictures of a world long past.

"But Grandmother," a small voice piped up, "if Clachanoch was so special, why did we leave it?"

Fyonna's smile wavered for a moment. She did not wish to burden young hearts with tales of mistakes and misfortunes, of greed and loss. Instead, she chose her words carefully.

"Sometimes, my dear, we must let go of the things we love in order to find new beginnings," she said. "Clachanoch's walls may stand empty now, but its spirit lives on in each of us. We carry its lessons, its stories, and its strength. And one day, who knows? Perhaps someone will return to it and bring new life to its halls."

One of the children, a thoughtful boy with a tuft of hair that refused to lie flat, looked up at her. "Could I go there one day? To Clachanoch?" he asked softly.

Fyonna placed a kiss on his forehead. "Aye, perhaps you will. And if you do, you'll take with you not just the name, but everything we stood for. Kindness. Honour. Courage."

The children nodded solemnly, the story settling into their hearts like seeds waiting to bloom. That evening, as they scattered to play and chase the last of the golden sunlight, Fyonna remained seated, her eyes gazing into the horizon, where the past and future seemed to blur.

Meanwhile, miles away, Alistair sat by his window, watching the evening light fade into dusk. An unexpected letter arrived from an old friend—Seamus O'Lally—who had heard of his struggles and wished to visit. Their reunion brought warmth to Alistair's heart, reminding him that even in solitude, one is never truly alone.

"You've more life left in you than you think, Alistair," Seamus told him one evening as they shared a quiet drink.

"Perhaps your days as Laird are gone, but that doesn't mean you have nothing left to give."

Alistair nodded, thoughtful. He had spent too long looking backwards, mourning what was lost. It was time to embrace the present and whatever days still lay ahead. With renewed purpose, he became more involved in the town, sharing his knowledge with those who sought it, offering guidance where he could. Though his legacy would not be written in the annals of noble history, it would be felt in the lives he touched, in the quiet acts of kindness that rippled through the generations.

On quiet evenings, he sometimes found himself walking the edge of the old path that once led to Clachanoch. Though he never followed it fully, he would pause and stare into the mist, letting the memories roll over him like the Highland winds. It was not grief that accompanied him now, but gratitude. For all he had seen, for all he had learned.

Yet, even as time moved forward, there were whispers of something left behind at Clachanoch. A presence unseen, lingering in the shadows of the abandoned manor. The wind that swept through the empty halls carried more than dust—it carried secrets, memories that refused to be forgotten. And somewhere, beyond the reach of those who once called it home, the estate waited.

In its stillness, Clachanoch endured. Through storms and silence, through sorrow and slumber, it remained. The ivy grew thicker, the floors creaked louder, and yet the bones of the house held firm. As if it knew its story was not yet finished.

For one day, in the distant future, a most unlikely descendant would return to Clachanoch.

And when they did, the echoes of the past would stir once more.

DOUGAL MCBETH

As the fire crackled and the warm glow illuminated the cosy room, Maree sat surrounded by her siblings—Caitriona, Isla, Ewan, and Fergus—along with Ewan's wife, Morag. The atmosphere brimmed with excitement and anticipation as they gathered to discuss Maree and Dougal's upcoming journey to Clachanoch Estate.

"I cannae believe you're actually going to do this," Isla exclaimed, her eyes shining. "To think, our own kin, uncovering the mysteries of their ancestors!"

"It's a grand adventure, to be sure," agreed Fergus. "And ye ken ye have us all behind ye, Maree. We'll take care of the croft and make sure everything runs smoothly while ye're away."

Maree smiled gratefully at her siblings, feeling a wave of emotion wash over her. "Thank ye, all of ye. We couldnae do this without yer support. Dougal and I are truly grateful."

Ewan raised his glass in a toast. "To Maree and Dougal—may yer journey be filled with wonder and discovery!"

In the days that followed, as preparations were made, Maree and Dougal approached Angus and Fiona, asking them to join them on the journey. The couple, who had travelled far and wide, eagerly accepted, thrilled at the prospect of uncovering the mysteries of Clachanoch Estate.

Their journey began in the soft light of dawn, the Highland landscape stretching before them in a breathtaking display of rolling moors and rugged peaks. Their horse-drawn buggies carried provisions—dried meats, oatcakes, cheese, nuts, and water, along with blankets and cooking supplies for the long road ahead.

Maree had spent her entire life in the village and on the croft, and she had never ventured beyond her familiar hills. Now, with each mile that passed, she felt as though she had stepped into another world—one filled with beauty and mystery beyond her imagination.

As they made their way through the moors, they passed herds of "hairy coos," their thick coats and curved horns making them look like creatures from a fairy tale. A family of red deer moved gracefully through the heather, their antlers catching the light in a golden hue. Maree gasped, clutching Dougal's arm. "Look at them, Dougal! They're just magnificent!"

Further along, a golden eagle soared overhead, its wide wings slicing through the sky. A kestrel hovered, scanning the ground for prey, while in the underbrush, a fox darted out of sight, its fiery coat a blur against the deep green of the ferns. Maree watched in wide-eyed wonder, drinking in every detail.

At one point, Fiona paused and pointed to a peculiar standing stone partially hidden among the bracken. "That there—it's no ordinary stone," she said. "There's old power in that shape. Almost like it's watchin' us pass." Angus nodded slowly, his brow furrowed. "Aye, I feel it too. Like it's a marker o' some sort—a boundary between past an' present." They lingered there for a moment in silence, each one quietly reverent of the ancient monolith, before continuing along the trail, their steps somehow lighter, their breaths a little more hushed.

At midday, they stopped by a crystal-clear loch to water the horses. Small ripples formed on the glassy surface as an otter slipped into the water, its sleek form disappearing beneath the reeds. "I didnae ken otters lived here," Maree murmured, her voice tinged with awe.

Angus chuckled. "Aye, they're the quiet guardians of these waters. If ye watch close, ye might see them playin'."

They boiled a pot over a small fire, sharing dark coffee and oatcakes before pressing on. The road wound through forests thick with pine, their scent filling the air. Owls perched high in the branches, their golden eyes watching as the travellers passed below.

They spent nights beneath a sky so vast it made Maree's heart ache with wonder. With no village lanterns to dim them, the stars stretched endlessly above, bright and endless. "It's like the heavens themselves have opened," she whispered, leaning against Dougal.

That night, as they camped near a gnarled old tree whose branches seemed to point toward the stars, Dougal awoke from a vivid dream. He sat up in silence, staring into the embers. In his dream, he had walked the halls of Clachanoch, but the rooms had been filled with whispers and shadowy figures. A voice—familiar yet unplaceable—had said, 'It isnae enough tae return. Ye must make it right.'

As they travelled, they stopped at small villages, resting the horses and gathering news. In one such village, they lodged at a thatched-roof inn where the innkeeper, a jovial man with a bushy beard, greeted them warmly.

"Clachanoch Estate, ye say? I've heard tales of that place—stories of grandeur and mystery. They say a Lowland woman once came and nearly bled it dry. Folk called her the Serpent in Silk—Vera, I believe. Weren't many sad to see her go."

The travellers exchanged glances, interest piqued.

"Ye'll be needing a good meal and a warm bed for the night. Come, sit by the fire and make yerselves comfortable."

The travellers enjoyed a hearty meal of roasted lamb, mashed potatoes, and fresh-baked bread, listening as the innkeeper shared legends passed down through the generations. The next morning, they set off early, the rising sun casting golden hues over the misty hills.

During one evening stop, Maree pulled out a bundle wrapped in linen—a letter from her mother, written many years ago in the final days of her illness. Though faded and creased, it was her most cherished keepsake, one she carried on every journey. As the fire crackled, she read the gentle words aloud to Dougal, her voice trembling slightly. 'Follow yer heart, my bairn, but never forget where ye come from.' He squeezed her hand, both of them feeling the weight of those words as a sacred reminder of what they were setting out to reclaim.

One afternoon, as they climbed a steep path overlooking the valley, Maree noticed movement on a distant ridge. "What's dat?" she asked, shading her eyes.

Fiona squinted. "A stag—an ole one by the looks of it."

The great beast stood atop the ridge, silhouetted against the sky. For a moment, he was perfectly still, watching them with dark, intelligent eyes before turning and vanishing into the trees.

Dougal exhaled slowly. "It's a sign. Dae land remembers."

Though his tone was soft, something deeper churned beneath. That phrase—*the land remembers*—lingered with him. His ancestors had walked this soil. Built on it. Bled for it. Misused it, perhaps. And now, he had returned not as a guest, but as its reckoner.

The air itself seemed to grow heavier the closer they came to the estate. Even the birds grew quiet, their chirping replaced by the rustle of leaves and the creak of ancient branches. Maree whispered, almost to herself, "It's like the land knows we're coming home." No one answered, but the silence that followed felt like agreement.

As they neared Clachanoch Estate, the landscape grew wilder. The trees were taller, their trunks thick with age, and the air carried the scent of damp earth and heather. They rode in silence, each absorbed in thought.

Finally, as they rounded a bend, the manor came into view—a grand but weather-worn structure nestled within the hills, its once-proud walls bearing the weight of time. Vines clung to the stone, and the windows, dark and hollow, seemed to watch their approach.

Maree's breath caught. "This is it."

Dougal reached for her hand. "Aye. And we're here tae reclaim what's ours."

But behind his words, there was a flicker of unease.

The stories were one thing.

Now, they were walking into them.

UNVEILING THE PAST

Dougal, Maree, Fiona, and Angus stood before the weathered gates of Clachanoch Estate, a quiet solemnity settled over them. The once-grand estate, though scarred by time and neglect, still exuded a quiet strength. Its ivy-laced towers bore the weight of history, each cracked stone whispering of lives lived and lost. Vines crept along the stone walls, and the gardens had grown wild, but the manor itself stood firm, its structure enduring despite the passage of time.

A soft breeze carried the scent of damp earth and heather, mingling with the distant call of a stag. Maree, wide-eyed, took in the towering trees that framed the estate, their ancient boughs whispering in the wind. The sight of the rolling moors and the rugged Highland landscape filled her with awe, as though she had stepped into a world beyond time.

As they stepped across the threshold, dust stirred beneath their feet, and the scent of aged wood and parchment filled the air. It felt less like they were exploring a house and more like being received by a silent observer. Clachanoch didn't just remember—it seemed to judge, to wait. The grandeur of the past was still evident in the manor's towering stone walls, the intricate carvings on the bannisters, and the vaulted ceilings that had stood the test of generations.

They wandered through the great hall, where a long banquet table, now draped in dust, stood as a reminder of the feasts once held within these walls. The tapestries that adorned the walls had faded, but the stories they depicted still whispered their ancient tales.

In the east wing, they discovered a vast library, its towering bookshelves filled with volumes untouched for decades. Dougal ran his fingers over the spines of old tomes, pausing at a weathered journal with the McBeth crest embossed on the cover. As he opened it, delicate handwriting revealed a glimpse into the thoughts of a past Laird, his words chronicling both prosperity and hardship.

In the west wing, they found the remains of a chapel, its stained glass windows still intact, though dulled by time. The light filtering through cast soft hues across the stone floor, illuminating an altar that had once served as the heart of Clachanoch's faith. Despite the silence that filled the space, there was a lingering sense of reverence, as if the echoes of prayers still hung in the air.

"Tis place holds so much hist'ry," Fiona murmured, her voice hushed with awe. "It's hard to believe yer ancestors once walked these halls."

Angus nodded, his keen eyes scanning the details of the architecture. "Aye, it's in need of care, but it's no' beyond saving."

Maree turned to Dougal, studying his expression as he gazed at the portrait of a past McBeth Laird. "What are ye thinking?" she asked gently.

Dougal exhaled, his brow furrowed. "I feel as though I was meant to be here," he admitted. "As if tis place was waitin' for mae to return."

They continued their exploration, uncovering locked doors and hidden alcoves. In one narrow corridor, Fiona stumbled upon a loose floorboard beneath a threadbare rug. When lifted, it revealed a shallow cavity containing a rusted iron key. "To what, I wonder?" she mused aloud. Dougal pocketed it carefully, a sense of anticipation tightening in his chest. "We'll find where it belongs soon enough," he said.

Later that afternoon, they entered a parlour choked with cobwebs, where a broken pianoforte rested beneath a dust-covered cloth. Maree gently lifted the edge, revealing ivory keys yellowed with age. "It's still beautiful," she whispered, striking a chord that echoed mournfully through the room. "Someone once played this for joy," Angus added, his voice distant. "Let's hope we can bring that joy back."

As the group explored the upper floors, a sudden gust of wind slammed a door shut behind them. Maree startled, clutching Dougal's arm. "It's just the wind," he said quickly, though his own heart raced. "Or the house remindin' us it's still alive," Fiona quipped, half-smiling. They laughed nervously, the sound strangely loud against the silence.

From a narrow window overlooking the rear of the estate, Angus pointed out what looked like the remnants of an old orchard. "Might be worth clearin' up," he said. "There's life under all that tangle—I can feel it." Dougal nodded, a flicker of hope lighting his expression. "Then we'll start there. One small piece at a time."

With a new sense of purpose, they left the manor and made their way toward the surrounding farmland, where they encountered an older farmer tending to a herd of shaggy Highland cattle. The man, his face weathered by years of working the land, greeted them with cautious curiosity.

"Ye'd be the McBeth lad, then," he remarked, leaning on his crook. "I heard ye were coming. My great-grandad worked for the McBeths—he saw it all before the doors shut for good."

Dougal nodded. "Aye. I was hoping to learn more about what happened to Clachanoch."

The farmer sighed, glancing toward the manor. "It's a story of fortune and folly, lad. Clachanoch was once the pride of the Highlands, but when Laird Alastair took over, things changed. He wed a woman, Vera—striking, ambitious, and sharp as a blade. Folk say she came wrapped in silk but carried iron beneath. She had no love for Clachanoch's ways, only for what it could become under her hand."

Dougal's jaw tensed. "An' what happened tae them?"

"Tey left when the debts overtook them," the farmer said. "Dae lawyers tried to salvage what dae could, but tae clause in the ole Laird's will—dat there was provision left, only if dae estate was managed wisely—was lost tae Alastair's failures. If Vera had known about it, perh'ps she would've reined in her spendin'. Or perh'ps not. She never settled for less t'an dae finest. Gold-rimmed crockery, imported silks... all while the roof began to cave in."

Maree's brow furrowed. "So there was a way Clachanoch could've been saved?"

The farmer nodded grimly. "Aye. But it was too late for them."

A wave of determination settled over Dougal. His ancestors had built this estate from the ground up, and though misfortune had nearly undone it, he was here now. He had returned, not to dwell on the mistakes of the past, but to reclaim what had been lost.

As they made their way back to the manor, the sun dipped low over the hills, casting long shadows across the land. A faint rustling in the nearby trees made Maree shiver.

"Did ye hear that?" she asked, glancing toward the edge of the woods.

Angus followed her gaze. "Aye. The wind, perhaps."

But as Dougal looked toward the gathering darkness, a strange unease settled in his chest. As though something—or someone—was watching. Nothing moved—but the feeling of being watched lingered, sharp as a thorn beneath the skin.

He shook the thought away. Whatever mysteries lay hidden within Clachanoch's walls, he would uncover them in due time. This was only the beginning.

THE DARKNESS OF HISTORY

The air inside Clachanoch Estate was thick with dust and time, the scent of aged parchment and faded memories lingering as Dougal, Maree, Fiona, and Angus delved into the heart of their family's past. The estate, though weathered, stood resilient against the passing centuries, holding secrets within its walls that had long been forgotten.

Dougal spent countless hours poring over old documents, ledgers, and letters, piecing together the intricate puzzle of his ancestors' lives. By candlelight, he traced the McBeth lineage, discovering stories of loyalty and betrayal, triumphs and tragedies—accounts that had shaped the family through the generations.

One evening, as they gathered in the great hall, Dougal unfolded a fragile letter written by Laird Alasdair McBeth to his son, Alastair. His voice was solemn as he read:

"Remember, son, that the strength of Clachanoch lies not in its wealth, but in its people. Treat them with respect and care, and the estate will thrive. Forget this, and all shall crumble."

Dougal's voice wavered as he finished. Maree noticed his hands trembling slightly.

Maree's eyes shimmered in the firelight. "He was a wise man. If only Alastair had listened."

Fiona nodded thoughtfully. "Tae past speaks to us in more ways than one. These stories hold lessons we cannae ignore."

Angus, ever the realist, leaned forward. "Aye, but we must also heed the warnings. The shadows of history are often as revealing as the light."

And shadows there were.

Among the records lay a tale of betrayal that had cast its long, dark reach over the McBeth name. Malcolm McBeth—a distant cousin, cunning and ambitious—had coveted the wealth and influence of the clan. Consumed by envy, he spread discord among the kin, whispering falsehoods and stirring division.

Malcolm's scheme culminated in a coup against Laird Alasdair McBeth, a beloved leader who had ruled with wisdom and justice. The ensuing conflict tore the clan apart, pitting brother against brother, friend against friend. Blood stained the halls of Clachanoch as Malcolm sought to claim power for himself.

But Alasdair, steadfast and unyielding, fought back with the support of his loyal kin. The traitor was ultimately vanquished, his name forever marked with disgrace. He fled into the wilderness, never to be seen again—yet his treachery left scars that never fully healed.

Beneath a loose floorboard in the library, Dougal uncovered an old velvet pouch containing a ceremonial dirk—its hilt engraved with the initials M.M.

"This must've been Malcolm's," he whispered.

Maree stepped back slightly. "It looks untouched."

"Tae sins o' the past linger," Dougal murmured, running a hand over the hilt. "T'is estate has known both greatness an' ruin."

Maree shivered. "And what've those who fell in dat battle? Their stories were nev'r told."

Fiona turned the pages of another old journal. "Perh'ps tey were nev'r meant to be."

The more they uncovered, the more Clachanoch revealed its ghosts.

There was the tale of Laird Graeme McBeth, a kind and generous leader who had taken in a band of weary travellers one bitter winter. He offered them shelter, unaware that among them lurked thieves who sought more than warmth and food.

Under the cover of night, they stole into the laird's chambers, taking with them a precious family heirloom—a necklace of Celtic design, passed down for generations. When Graeme awoke to find it gone, he was consumed with grief and rage. He set out into the Highlands in pursuit, determined to reclaim what had been lost.

His journey ended in bloodshed. Outnumbered and ambushed, Graeme was struck down, left to perish beneath the shadow of the mountains. The necklace was never recovered, whispered of in legend, cursed to bring misfortune to any who possessed it.

One morning, Maree discovered a bundle of dried herbs tucked behind a loose brick in the scullery. Alongside it was a small scrap of parchment with an old healing chant written in Gaelic. "Someone here practised folk medicine," she said quietly. "Likely in secret." Fiona examined it with interest. "Aye, could've been a servant or even a laird's wife—someone who healed in the shadows when the kirk looked down on it."

One afternoon, while sifting through a trunk in the attic, Dougal unearthed a bundle of letters tied with a faded ribbon.

"Taese wer' exchanged between Laird Alasdair an' his brother, Doonan," he said, his brow furrowed. "Tey speak o' economic hardship, o' debts threatening tae swallow tae estate."

Maree peered over his shoulder. "Tey worked so hard tae hold it togeth'r."

Later, Fiona found a faded page tucked between two hymnals in the chapel. It was a child's drawing—charcoal on linen—showing the estate and a small figure beside it marked with the name 'Ailsa.' Maree traced the name with a fingertip. "I wonder who she was," she whispered. "Someone who once called this home... someone who mattered."

Days later, Fiona, studying an old map, pointed at markings in faded ink. "Look at tis—hidden rooms. Passageways. Secrets still waitin' tae be found."

Their search led them deeper into the manor, tapping at walls and prying at floorboards until a discovery halted them in their tracks. Behind a loose panel in the library, Angus uncovered a concealed staircase spiralling into darkness.

Lanterns in hand, they descended, their breaths shallow as they entered a long-forgotten chamber.

A sharp creak echoed above them, as if the house itself were shifting in response to their descent.

The room was lined with shelves laden with ledgers and ancient tomes. At the centre stood an ornate chest, its lock rusted but still intact. Dougal forced it open, revealing a velvet-lined box nestled within.

Inside, resting as though untouched by time, was the lost necklace of Laird Graeme McBeth.

Maree gasped. "It cannae be."

Dougal ran his fingers over the intricate silverwork. "It matches tae description in Graeme's journal. It were hidden here all alon'."

Fiona stepped closer, her expression softened with awe. "He was a man who gave freely an' withoot fear. I see him in tis. In what we're tryin' to do."

"Dae past isn't finished wit' us yet," Fiona murmured.

In the same chamber, Angus stumbled across a crate sealed with wax, long forgotten behind a collapsed shelf. Inside were several hand-forged tools, a child's wooden toy, and a journal belonging to a steward named Callum. His entries described sleepless nights keeping watch during the estate's darker days. "He guarded this place even as it crumbled," Angus said, his voice low. "Some folk stayed behind when others fled."

But of all the stories they unearthed, none were as tragic as that of Imogen McBeth.

A young woman of kindness and beauty, Imogen had fallen in love with Errol, a farmer of humble means. Their love defied class and convention, a bond stronger than the barriers imposed by wealth and status.

Her father, Laird Alexander McBeth, forbade the union. Yet the lovers continued to meet in secret, their hearts defiant against the world.

One fateful night, fire engulfed the manor. The flames consumed the great hall, trapping Imogen inside. Errol, upon hearing her cries, rushed in, fighting against the inferno to reach her.

He carried her to safety—but neither survived their injuries.

The fire was no accident.

No culprit was ever named, but whispers echoed through the years. Some said it was the laird himself, determined to separate them at any cost. Others claimed it was an act of vengeance, carried out by a jealous suitor.

But the truth, like the ashes of that fateful night, had long since scattered with the wind.

While tidying a seldom-used cabinet near the charred remnants of the east wing, Maree found a folded slip of paper hidden behind a broken tile.

It was a letter:

To my beloved Imogen,

If this reaches you, know that I would cross fire itself to find you again. They will never understand what we share. But my heart is yours, always. If fate separates us, I will find you in the next life.

—Errol

Maree pressed the note to her chest, her eyes misting. "He meant ever' word."

Later, Fiona lit a candle in the ruined chapel and placed the note at the foot of the altar. "For their peace," she said softly. Maree joined her, head bowed, the flame dancing gently beside them as if in reverent approval. The chapel, for a fleeting moment, felt whole again.

As Dougal stood among the ruins of the past, he realised that Clachanoch was not merely a place of grandeur—it was a monument to sacrifice, to love and loss, to the choices that shaped a legacy.

"We must preserve t'ese stories," he said at last. "No' just the good, but tae painful ones too. They belong to us."

Angus nodded. "Aye. To know where we're goin', we must first ken where we've been."

Maree placed a hand on Dougal's arm, her touch grounding him. "An' where we are noo," she said softly. "Clachanoch still stands. Dat means its story isn't over."

Fiona glanced toward the darkened corridor, where shadows seemed to shift in the dim light. "No' yet, at least."

As they left the chamber behind, the air in the manor seemed heavier, as though something unseen had stirred.

And somewhere, in the veiled recesses of Clachanoch, history watched and waited.

Despite the darkness of its history—and the burden Dougal now felt pressing against his heart—he was ready. Ready to bear the name McBeth into a new age. Not to repeat the past, but to transform it.

THE DOCUMENTS OF THE LAND

As the morning light filtered through the ancient trees surrounding Clachanoch Estate, Maree turned to Dougal, her expression thoughtful. "Dougal, we've been here a fair bit now, and ye've unearthed so much about Clachanoch Estate. What d'ye think our next steps should be?"

Dougal nodded, his gaze focused. "Aye, Maree, I've been ponderin' that. If we're tae bide here and make it our own, we need tae do it legally and in the right way. I reckon we should head into the village and see if there's a local office where historical land records are kept. We'll need tae find out about title deeds, land transfers, and property ownership information."

"That sounds like a plan," Maree agreed. "Fiona and Angus can keep an eye on things here while we're gone. It'll be guid tae have some official confirmation o' our rights tae the estate."

Dougal smiled, a glint of excitement in his eyes. "Exactly. And who kens, we might unearth even more about the history o' this place. It's been quite the journey so far, has it no'?"

"It certainly has, Dougal," Maree replied, returning his smile. "But I'm glad we're in this together. Let's head tae the village and see what we can find out."

The journey to the village was filled with a mix of anticipation and determination. Dougal and Maree were greeted by the sight of quaint stone cottages and winding streets. The village was small but bustling, with locals going about their daily business. The atmosphere was warm and inviting, a stark contrast to the weighty matters they were there to address.

As they passed a baker's shop, the woman behind the counter, flour-dusted and bright-eyed, stepped outside. "Clachanoch, ye say? I thought that place was cursed tae crumble," she said with a curious glance. "Good luck tae ye both, then. Perhaps ye'll be the ones tae turn it around."

They smiled politely and continued on, feeling the watchful eyes of a village that remembered the estate's decline all too well.

They soon located the local office that housed the historical land records. Stepping inside, they were greeted by the musty smell of old books and documents. A friendly clerk, a middle-aged man with round glasses and a welcoming smile, greeted them and asked how he could assist.

"We're here tae inquire aboot the historical records o' Clachanoch Estate," Dougal explained. "We're lookin' for information on title deeds, land transfers, and property ownership."

The clerk nodded, his interest piqued. "Clachanoch Estate, ye say? A place with a rich history, indeed. Follow me, and I'll show ye where we keep our records."

He led them to a dimly lit room filled with shelves of documents, maps, and old ledgers. The air was thick with the scent of aged paper and ink. "These records go back centuries," he said, gesturing to the shelves. "Ye might find what ye're lookin' for here."

Among the stacks, Maree spotted a folio bearing the McBeth crest. "This one looks promising," she said, pulling it carefully from the shelf. Inside were correspondence letters between the McBeths and local officials about boundary disputes, estate matters, and even an old invoice for the chapel's restoration after a storm in 1792. "It's like touching a thread from the past," she whispered.

After hours of searching through dusty ledgers and faded papers, their eyes fell upon a set of documents that seemed to hold the key to Clachanoch's future. These papers, bearing the official seal of the estate, detailed the transfer of ownership from the McBeth family to a distant relative named Robert McAllister. The entries were meticulous, recording every transaction and legal detail with care.

As they pored over the records, Maree's heart raced with anticipation. Could this be the evidence they needed to reclaim Clachanoch Estate? She could hardly believe they had finally found something concrete after all their searching. Dougal, too, felt a surge of excitement, realising that they were on the brink of unravelling a mystery that had haunted his dreams for so long.

A heavy silence settled as they turned the final page. "It says here that the solicitor kept a lockbox for safekeeping," Dougal murmured. "Might still be held with the clerk's office or passed to an archive." Maree's eyes lit up. "If we find that box, it could hold everything we need."

However, their elation was short-lived as they discovered a troubling detail in the records. Despite inheriting the estate, Robert McAllister had never claimed it. According to the documents, he had passed away without any known descendants or heirs. This meant that Clachanoch had reverted back to the lawyer who, for generations, had held it in trust for a living descendant who would come forward.

The realisation hit them like a blow. The estate, which had been their beacon of hope, now seemed further out of reach than ever before. Dougal sat in silence, the old ledger open on the table. "Was I ever meant tae reclaim this place at all?" he whispered.

Maree reached for his hand, her voice firm. "Ye were. We're just not done yet."

To prove their lineage and rightful claim to Clachanoch Estate, Dougal and Maree turned to their own family records, searching for any documents that could link them to Robert McAllister or provide clues about their ancestry. As they continued their efforts, they reached out to Maree's sister Caitriona for help. Caitriona, a schoolteacher with a knack for research, eagerly agreed to assist. Soon, she, along with Isla, Ewan, Morag, and Fergus, as well as Elspeth, made their way to Clachanoch Estate.

As they arrived, their breath was taken away by the sheer size and grandeur of the manor and its surrounding lands. "Oh, my word," Isla exclaimed. "I had no idea it was so... magnificent!"

"Aye, 'tis a sight to behold," Ewan agreed. "Imagine the stories these walls could tell."

Fergus beamed. "It's a testament to the strength and resilience of your ancestors, Dougal. To think that this estate has been in your family for generations—it's truly remarkable."

Caitriona set up her small workspace in the study, quickly pulling together research leads and old census records. "We'll need to speak with the parish minister. The Kirk records will likely be key," she said, flipping through her notebook.

With the help of local historians, parish clerks, archivists, and legal professionals, they discovered birth certificates, marriage records, and other vital documents that supported their claim, tracing their ancestry back to the McBeth family. To strengthen their case legally, they enlisted the help of a solicitor specialising in inheritance law.

During one trip to the local kirk, Angus found a weathered gravestone tucked behind overgrown vines—its inscription nearly worn away. "Aye, this might be the missing link," he said, brushing the moss aside. Maree took a photo, her heart pounding. "We're closer than ever now."

After weeks of diligent research and preparation, Dougal and Maree were ready to present their case. Armed with a wealth of evidence, they approached the authorities responsible for overseeing the estate's transfer of ownership. The process was arduous, filled with legal complexities and historical intricacies. At one point, a stern council official eyed their documentation with suspicion. "It's nae a small thing, claiming land of that size," he said. "Ye'll need to be thorough."

They were.

Finally, after some intense deliberation, the authorities recognised their claim as legitimate. Dougal and Maree were declared the rightful heirs to Clachanoch Estate, reclaiming the legacy that had been lost to their family for generations.

As the official documents were signed, Dougal turned to Maree, his eyes filled with emotion. "We've done it, Maree. Clachanoch is ours."

Maree smiled, tears of joy streaming down her cheeks. "Aye, Dougal. We've reclaimed your heritage. Your ancestors would be proud."

Fiona and Angus joined them, their faces reflecting the same sense of pride and fulfilment. "This is just the beginning," Fiona said. "We have much work ahead to restore the estate, but we're ready for it."

Angus nodded in agreement. "Together, we'll bring Clachanoch back to its former glory."

That evening, they raised glasses of whisky in the great hall. The fire crackled in the hearth, laughter echoing through walls that had known only silence for too long.

Elspeth stood at the edge of the room, watching with quiet pride. Her eyes gleamed with something ancient and knowing.

The past had finally made peace with the present.

And as Dougal looked toward the cold, broken chapel in the distance, he knew one thing:

Their journey had only just begun.

MORMAER OF MORAY

With the title deed finally secured and their rightful ownership of Clachanoch Estate confirmed, Dougal, Maree, Fiona, and Angus stood at the threshold of a new beginning. Though the battle for their heritage had been long and fraught with challenges, the moment of victory had arrived. Yet, as they prepared to return to their crofts, there was an unshakable feeling that this was only the beginning of something much greater.

Before leaving, Dougal lingered at the edge of the orchard. The last light of day kissed the crumbling stone walls, and he stood still, breathing it all in. Clachanoch was theirs. But in the hush of dusk, he felt a hum beneath the earth, as though the stones themselves were holding their breath. The wind carried a scent of moss and distant smoke, and for a moment, it seemed to speak.

Packing up their belongings, they took one last look at the estate that had so profoundly changed their lives. The walls of Clachanoch seemed to stand taller now, no longer a place of uncertainty but a home reclaimed. Though there was much work ahead to restore it fully, it was now undeniably theirs.

"Aye, we'll be back soon," Maree declared, her voice brimming with determination. "And when we do, we'll be ready to face whatever lies ahead."

With that, they turned and made their way back to their buggies, ready to return to their crofts for now, but with their hearts set on the journey that lay ahead.

As they neared their beloved crofts, the familiar landscape opened up before them. The rolling hills, the scent of heather on the crisp Highland air, and the welcoming glow of home filled them with a deep sense of contentment. It was as if the land itself rejoiced at their return, embracing them in its timeless grasp. As they crested the last rise, they could see the chimney smoke curling up from the Doonagan croft, a sign that all was well. The sheep dotted the hillside, and someone—perhaps Isla or Caitriona—had hung linens to dry between two hawthorn trees. It was a view that made Dougal's heart clench with gratitude.

If by some unspoken agreement, Elspeth was there to greet them. The silver-haired matron stood amidst the blooming heather, the setting sun casting an ethereal glow around her. Her presence had always been a source of wisdom and comfort, a bridge between the past and the present.

Their siblings rushed out to meet them, their faces alight with joy and curiosity. The warmth of home surrounded them as they stepped inside the croft, where a hearty meal awaited. Around the table, they shared stories of their journey—of the hardships faced, the victories won, and the mysteries yet to be unravelled.

The evening stretched on and the fire crackled in the hearth, Elspeth's sharp eyes sparkled with intrigue. There was something she had long wished to share, something that might deepen their understanding of Clachanoch and the history that bound them to it.

Before she spoke, Elspeth rose and retrieved a carved wooden box from beneath the sideboard. It was old and worn smooth with time, but the clasp still held firm. "This," she said, placing it on the table, "was passed tae me by my own grandmother. It belonged tae her grandfather's grandfather—who claimed his lineage from tae northern lords of Moray."

"Long ago," she began, her voice a soft murmur carrying the weight of centuries, "afore the stones of Clachanoch were laid, dat land was a place of great import'nce. It was here dat tae Mormaer o' Moray held court, ruling o'er tese lands wit' wisdom an' strength."

A hush fell over the room as everyone leaned in to listen, the flickering fire casting shifting shadows on the walls.

"In tose days," she continued, "tae province o' Moray was a battleground, a place where Scottish an' Norse forces clashed fir control. The Mormaer was more than a ruler; he was a warrior, a guardian o' his people against tae tide o' invaders dat sought ta claim tese lands."

Her words painted vivid images in their minds: warriors standing resolute upon the Highland moors, shields locked in defiance against encroaching forces. The clang of swords and the roar of battle seemed to echo from the past, filling the silence of the croft.

"Tae fortress dat once stood t'ere was a stronghold, built ta withstand tae test o' time an' tae might o' enemies. But as tae centuries passed, tae power o' tae Mormaer waned, an' tae fortress fell into ruin. Its walls crumbled, its halls emptied, and tae echoes o' its glory faded int' legend. O'er time, the land was o'ertaken by wild brambles, trees, an' thick undergrowth. Tae ruins disappeared beneath tae grasp o' nature, swallowed by time itself." Angus shifted uncomfortably. "Are ye tellin' us Clachanoch was built atop a battlefield?" Elspeth gave a slow nod. "Aye, and not just any battleground—but one soaked in both honour an' sorrow. Dae bones o' heroes and traitors alike rest beneath tae heather."

Maree's breath caught in her throat. "And Clachanoch was built upon tase ver' ruins?"

Elspeth nodded. "Aye, the stones of the manor bear witness t' tae struggles an' triumphs of tose who came before. The land remembers, even when men forget."

A deep, reverent silence settled over the room. The weight of history pressed upon them—not as a burden, but as an inheritance waiting to be honoured.

Then, with a knowing glint in her eyes, Elspeth leaned forward. "T'ere are whispers—old stories—o' somethin' more buried within Clachanoch's grounds. Not gold nor jewels, but somethin' far greater. Knowledge. Power. Secrets passed doon from tose who first walked tis land."

Dougal felt a chill run down his spine, the whispers in his dreams suddenly making more sense.

"What kin' a knowledge?" Angus asked, his usual scepticism giving way to curiosity.

"It is said," Elspeth whispered, "dat tae original occupants o' tis land left behind writin's o' ald wisdom—knowledge o' tae stars, tae earth, an' tae mysteries o' creation itself. Tese were entrusted to tae Mormaer, a sacred duty to protect and use tem for tae good o' his people."

Maree exchanged a glance with Dougal. "If tese writin's exist... dae could change everyt'ing."

Elspeth nodded. "Aye. But dae are hidden, as all true treasures are. And tae land does not give up its secrets easily."

That night, while most had gone tae sleep, Fiona stepped out beneath the stars. Her hands rested on the cool stone wall of the croft as she looked northward. "Ye ken," she whispered to herself, "I can feel them watchin'. The ancients. Like they're waitin' for us to understand somethin' we've missed."

That night, long after the others had gone to bed, Dougal sat awake by the fire, the warmth crackling around him as he dozed off in his chair. In his dreams, he stood in a vast hall of stone, lit by flaming torches. Warriors knelt before a cloaked figure seated on a high seat of carved granite—the Mormaer of Moray.

The Mormaer's voice echoed in the chamber. "Ye bear oor name. Ye walk oor land. Dannae forget what it cost tae keep i' safe."

Dougal reached out—but the dream dissolved into mist.

He woke with a start, the fire now embers. The wind howled outside, rattling the windows. But in his heart, he knew. The journey they thought they had completed was only just beginning. Whatever lay ahead, they would face it together—as the new guardians of Clachanoch.

As he looked out into the dark, the land beyond the croft whispered promises not yet fulfilled. And somewhere, in the veiled recesses of the Highlands, the Mormaer's legacy stirred once more.

FAREWELL TO THE CROFT

As the sun dipped below the horizon, casting a golden glow over the rolling hills of the Highlands, Dougal sat outside his croft, the familiar scent of heather and peat smoke filling the air. Maree joined him, her eyes reflecting the flickering flames of the fire.

"Dougal, ye seem troubled," Maree observed, settling beside him. "What's weighin' on yer mind?"

Dougal sighed, his gaze fixed on the distant silhouette of Clachanoch Estate. "I love our croft, Maree. Ye ken that. But the call of Clachanoch grows stronger by the day. I feel as though I'm bein' pulled in two different directions."

Maree took his hand in hers, offering silent support. "Ye have a deep connection to that land, Dougal. It's in yer blood. But our croft is our home, where we've built our life together. It's no' an easy decision, I ken."

"I ken, Maree. But I feel as though there's somethin' waitin' for me at Clachanoch, somethin' I need tae discover," Dougal said, his voice filled with uncertainty.

Maree squeezed his hand gently. "Then we'll discover it together, Dougal. Whatever ye decide, I'll be by yer side."

Dougal smiled, a sense of peace settling over him. "Thank ye, Maree. I dinnae ken what I'd do without ye."

"We'll figure it out, Dougal. We always do," Maree replied, her voice full of conviction.

As twilight deepened, the wind picked up and carried with it the scent of change. It tugged at Maree's shawl and rustled the ivy on the croft walls. Even the sheep grew quiet as though they too sensed the turning of a chapter. The land itself seemed to listen.

That night, as Dougal drifted into sleep, the swirling winds seemed to whisper to him in a language only his heart could understand. Visions of Clachanoch Estate filled his dreams—its halls whispering tales of the past, of battles fought and lost, of love and loss. When he awoke, he knew what he had to do.

As the morning broke, Dougal packed a small wooden box carved by his father, lifting the lid to find a worn leather-bound journal and a compass that had belonged to his grandfather. He tucked them into his satchel—symbols of guidance and memory.

Later that morning, Maree wandered out alone into the moors. The sky was silver and quiet, the air full of mist. She made her way to the standing stones near the edge of the fields—ancient, lichen-covered, and solemn.

She placed her hand on one of the stones. "Mam, Da... I'm goin'. Me and Dougal—we're leavin' the crofts. Headin' tae Clachanoch. I hope ye'd be proud. I'll carry ye with me. Always."

She left a sprig of heather tucked into the stone's crevice, then turned back toward the croft.

Later that morning, Maree sought out Elspeth, finding the old woman seated on a weathered bench outside her croft, weaving a garland of wildflowers with deft fingers.

"Come now, lass," Elspeth said without looking up, a knowing glint in her eye. "Ye've that look about ye. The one that says ye've been listenin' too hard to the wind and not enough to yer own heart."

Maree huffed a small laugh and sat beside her. "And what if the wind's been makin' more sense than me own thoughts?"

Elspeth chuckled, tucking a sprig of lavender behind Maree's ear. "Ach, then ye must be listenin' wrong! The earth doesnae whisper nonsense, child. It hums with truth—ye just have to ken how to hear it right."

Maree sighed. "I just wonder if I'm truly ready. If I can hear it as ye do."

Elspeth nudged her shoulder. "Och, of course ye are. If ye were any more attuned to the land, I'd be worried ye'd start growin' roots yerself."

Maree let out a laugh, shaking her head. "Ye always have a way of makin' me feel foolish and wise all at once."

Elspeth grinned. "That's me talent, dear one. But truly, ye've got the gift. The land speaks to ye, same as it does to me. And ye'll hear it clearer than ever at Clachanoch. That place is alive with echoes of the past, aye? If ye listen close enough, it might just tell ye what ye need to know."

She reached into her pocket and handed Maree a smooth black stone etched with ancient markings. "Take this. It's been passed down through the wise women o' our line. Keep it with ye. The earth remembers, aye... but it also chooses what it forgets."

Maree met Elspeth's gaze, a warmth spreading through her chest. "Then I suppose I'd best be ready to listen."

Elspeth smirked, handing her the finished garland. "Aye, but mind ye don't let it talk ye into too much trouble, lass. The land's got a wicked sense of humour when it fancies."

Maree laughed and tucked the garland into her hair. "I'll try, but no promises."

Nearby, Isla had gathered the younger children to help prepare a send-off supper. As they peeled potatoes and braided flowers into loops, she watched them with a mix of fondness and sadness. The croft would feel different without Maree. Empty, perhaps—but also full of stories yet to be written.

That evening, while the sky still clung to the last of its twilight, Ewan and Morag sat on the bench behind their croft. A candle burned low on the windowsill beside them, casting soft light across their faces.

"Ye sure about this, love?" Ewan asked, his voice low.

Morag didn't answer immediately. She stared out over the familiar hills, then turned to him. "Aye. I am.

It's no' just about followin' them—it's about findin' somethin' for us. A new beginning."

Ewan wrapped an arm around her shoulders. "I never thought we'd leave these hills. But there's somethin' stirrin' at Clachanoch. I feel it in my bones. Maybe it's time we made our mark somewhere else."

Morag leaned into him. "Together, then."

Just after dusk, a heavy mist rolled down the glen, curling around the croft buildings like a slow-moving river. Elspeth watched it from her window, murmuring an old rhyme under her breath. "When mist returns tae Highland floor, new paths shall open, old wounds restore."

The next morning, their decision set, Dougal and Maree called together their friends and family to share the news. The group gathered in the warm glow of the croft, listening intently.

"We've decided to heed the call of Clachanoch Estate," Dougal announced. "We're goin' to explore its mysteries and uncover its secrets. But this time, we're stayin' for good."

Fiona and Angus, adventurers at heart, were quick to offer their support. "To think of all the history and stories waitin' to be discovered!" Fiona exclaimed. Angus nodded. "Aye, it'll be quite the adventure. And who kens what we'll find there!"

Morag and Ewan exchanged a glance before stepping forward. Ewan cleared his throat and addressed Dougal and

Maree directly. "Dougal, Maree... if ye'll have us, we'd like tae come tae Clachanoch too. We want tae help rebuild it—and live there, if there's space for us."

Dougal and Maree looked at each other, their eyes lighting with joy. Dougal grinned. "Och, of course we'll have ye! We'd be honoured tae have ye both there wi' us."

Maree added, her voice warm, "It wouldnae feel right without the two o' ye. There's plenty o' room at Clachanoch—and plenty o' work tae share."

Others weighed in—some eager to join, others content to stay behind. Fergus, comfortable with his life at the croft, patted Angus on the back. "I'll hold down the fort here. Ye go and have yer adventure, and bring back stories for us to share."

Caitriona, devoted to her work at the local school, chose to stay as well. "But I'll be awaitin' yer return, eager to hear all about yer discoveries."

As the sun set on their last evening at the crofts, the entire community gathered for a grand send-off. Tables were laid with dishes of venison stew, bannocks hot from the griddle, honeyed oatcakes, and roasted root vegetables. Candles flickered in jars, casting soft light over the flowers woven into garlands.

Children wove paper stars and hung them from the eaves of the croft. One by one, they whispered wishes into the folded points—dreams for the journey ahead. Some asked for courage, others for adventure. And a few, shyly, asked for stories.

Isla took up her fiddle and played a tune that swelled with warmth and bittersweet joy. Children danced in circles, old folk raised their glasses, and the air buzzed with love and farewells.

Caitriona found Maree by the fire, watching the flames flicker.

"So, ye're really off then," Caitriona said, nudging her shoulder.

"Aye. Dinnae think I'll sleep tonight."

Caitriona handed her a wrapped bundle. "It's Mum's old shawl. I thought ye should have it."

Maree's breath caught. "Ye daft cow, ye'll have me cryin'."

"Ye've cried harder over peelie-wally stews," Caitriona said, pulling her into a fierce hug. "Go make somethin' new, lass. But don't forget where ye came from."

Isla then pulled Maree aside for a quiet moment at the edge of the firelight. "I'm no guid at this sort o' thing, ye ken," she said with a small smile. "But I'll miss ye, Maree. The place won't be the same without ye."

Maree wrapped her in a hug. "And I'll miss ye too, more than ye ken. But I promise—I'll write. And when we settle in, ye'll have a room waitin', always."

Isla nodded, her voice thick. "Ye'd better. Or I'll be showin' up wi' me fiddle and no warnin'."

The two sisters laughed, holding onto each other a moment longer.

As the celebration swelled around them, Dougal stepped quietly into the dark. He wandered to the edge of the field and placed a hand on the ancient stone wall, gazing up at the stars.

"Ah ken ye're watchin'," he whispered. "We'll do it right this time. We'll make ye proud."

Behind him, laughter spilt from the croft, firelight dancing on the windows.

Clachanoch awaited.

And they were ready.

HOME, SWEET MANOR

The group of six arrived back at Clachanoch Estate, a sense of excitement and anticipation filling the air. The journey had been long, but they were finally here, ready to begin their new adventure. The estate lay before them, a sprawling expanse of land and buildings that seemed to hold endless possibilities.

Morag and Ewan sat still atop the buggy, staring wide-eyed. Neither had ever seen anything quite like Clachanoch. Morag's mouth parted slightly. "Saints above... it's massive."

Ewan nodded slowly, trying to take it all in. "I thought my mind was exaggeratin' last time! But this—it's like somethin' from a storybook."

The towering stone facade rose before them like a fortress, its shadow stretching long over the land. Though worn by time and weather, the manor stood proud.

"We're no' just fixin' up a house," Morag murmured, eyes still wide. "This place... it's a world."

Maree smiled. "Aye, and now it's ours."

Maree, with a smile on her face, handed the front door key to Dougal. The key was large and rusty, a testament to the age of the manor. With a bit of effort, Dougal managed to wiggle the key into the lock and turn it, unlocking the door with a satisfying click. With a grand gesture, he swung the door open, marking the first time they stepped inside as its rightful owners.

Filled with a sense of tradition, Dougal picked up Maree in his arms and carried her over the threshold, a gesture that was met with laughter and applause from Angus, Fiona, Ewan, and Morag. It was a moment of joy and celebration, marking the beginning of their new life at Clachanoch Estate.

Ewan and Morag stood just inside the door, their eyes wide with awe. Morag whispered, "By the saints... it's even grander than I remembered."

Ewan turned slowly on the spot, taking in the vaulted ceilings, the grand staircase, and the lingering scent of woodsmoke and old stone. "This place... it's massive. There's just the six o' us?"

Maree grinned. "Aye. Welcome tae Clachanoch. And get ready—we've work tae do."

Having explored the manor before, they were no strangers to its grandeur, its hidden corners, and its many secrets. But until now, they had not truly called it home. Before securing ownership, they had lived in makeshift tents behind the manor, hesitant to claim what was not yet legally theirs. Now, with the deed in their hands, they were free to explore every inch of the estate.

Their first night sleeping indoors was oddly quiet. No rustling tent canvas. No wind snapping ropes. Just the long sigh of the old house settling around them. The stone walls held the day's chill, and the wind moaned softly through the chimneys.

Maree lay awake a while, hand resting on Dougal's chest. "It doesnae quite feel like home yet," she whispered.

"Nae," he replied. "But it will."

The next morning, they set to work.

Dougal and Maree claimed a room that had once belonged to a past Laird and Lady. The four-poster bed creaked with age but felt like a throne compared to the hard ground they'd camped on. Fiona wandered the corridors by moonlight, unable to sleep, her footsteps echoing off cold stone. Morag nestled into bed beside Ewan, murmuring, "This place is so quiet, it feels like it's listenin'."

The upper rooms, once untouched out of respect, now lay before them as a new realm of discovery. The grand four-poster beds and elegant drapery of the bedrooms beckoned them. The children's nursery, with its faded murals and antique toys, whispered of long-forgotten laughter. The servants' quarters, simple yet warm, held echoes of those who had cared for Clachanoch through the ages.

As they moved through these newly accessible spaces, a renewed sense of purpose settled over them. With their legal ownership established, they were ready to fully embrace the legacy of Clachanoch Estate.

Angus, Dougal, and Ewan took on the task of assessing the manor's interior, room by room, making note of structural damage, rotting floorboards, and ageing chimneys clogged with bird nests. The fireplaces, crucial for warmth in the frigid Highland winters, needed urgent repairs.

The women—Maree, Fiona, and Morag—assisted where they could, often with comical results. When the men disturbed a particularly large nest, a sudden flurry of birds sent them all scattering, shrieks of laughter ringing through the halls. Fiona, brushing feathers from her skirt, declared, "Well, that's one way tae wake the spirits."

It was Fiona who discovered a narrow servant's stair they'd previously overlooked. Hidden behind a warped panel, the tiny staircase curved steeply down into the west wing.

"Would ye look at that," she murmured, brushing cobwebs from her hair. "How many secrets does this place still hold?"

But it was the chapel that stopped them all cold.

They had known it was in poor shape, but nothing could have prepared them for the sight. The stained-glass windows had been shattered, their brilliant colours dulled to jagged shards on the stone floor. Pews lay broken and overturned. Sacred objects were strewn like debris.

Morag stepped forward, mouth tight. "Who would do this?"

Ewan ran a hand along the altar's scorched edge. "Someone wi' no respect for what this place meant."

Dougal crouched and gathered the broken glass into a pile. "We'll fix it. No' just for us, but for what it stood for."

They spent the rest of the day cleaning the chapel in silence, each moved by their own quiet sorrow and determination.

That night, after dinner, Dougal wandered alone down the hall, guided by candlelight. He entered what had once been the nursery. The murals, though faded, still danced across the walls. A rocking horse stood in the corner. Dust motes floated in the air like memory.

He stood quietly, absorbing it all. "We'll make ye proud," he whispered to the silence.

Elsewhere, Maree wandered the chapel alone. She lit a small candle and knelt before the altar. "Help us build somethin' worth leavin' behind," she murmured. "Let this be more than stone and timber. Let it be true."

They discovered more secrets within the manor. Behind a fallen bookshelf in the library, Fiona unearthed a hidden compartment containing old manuscripts and letters. That evening, she read aloud a passage by candlelight:

"...And though the world outside grows colder, within these walls we preserve more than stone—we preserve memory, duty, and soul."

Silence followed, broken only by the fire's soft crackle.

"That's what we're doin' now," Dougal said quietly. "We're preservin' its soul."

The discovery stirred something in all of them. These were not just curiosities—they were connections. To those who had come before, and to each other.

Outside, the work was just as demanding. The once-manicured gardens had been swallowed by overgrowth, the fields lay fallow, and the livestock pens were in disrepair. Ewan, Morag, and Angus dedicated themselves to clearing the land and preparing it for planting, determined to return the estate to its former glory.

One afternoon, Morag stood at the edge of a moss-covered stone wall, wiping her brow. "How in the world did they manage all this, centuries ago?"

Ewan stepped beside her, surveying the expanse. "They had an army. We've got six."

Morag smiled faintly. "Then we'd better be mighty."

As the days turned into weeks, Clachanoch Estate began to breathe again. The gardens flourished, the fields were ploughed, and the chapel, with its slowly restored stained-glass windows, stood as a beacon of renewal.

One afternoon, a curious visitor arrived—a wiry farmer from the neighbouring Glen.

"Heard the place was breathin' again," he said, tipping his cap. "Thought I'd come see for meself."

Dougal welcomed him inside. The man whistled low at the progress. "Lot o' folk said Clachanoch was cursed. Good tae see someone's provin' 'em wrong."

That evening, as they sat by the fire, Dougal, Angus, and Ewan discussed the pressing repairs needed before winter.

"We need tae get those upper rooms sorted," Angus said, his brow furrowed. "The roof is sound, but the windows and walls need fixin'."

Ewan nodded. "Aye, and we cannae forget about the floors. Some are so rotten, they'll need replacing altogether."

Dougal sighed. "We've already used up the funds we set aside. We'll need tae find another way tae get more money for the repairs."

A contemplative silence fell between them, the firelight flickering in their thoughtful expressions. It was Ewan who finally broke the quiet.

"It's a lot, aye. More than I ever thought I'd be takin' on. Feels strange sometimes, knowin' this place belongs tae us now. Feels... heavy."

Angus nodded, staring into his mug. "Aye. It's no' just a house. It's history. A legacy. An' we've got the weight o' all that on our shoulders."

Dougal took a long breath, leaning back. "I ken what ye mean. I always wanted tae make somethin' of myself. Prove I could do more than just get by. But this? This is bigger than any of us. An' sometimes I wonder if we've bitten off more than we can chew."

Ewan glanced at him. "Ye regret it?"

Dougal shook his head. "Nae. But it scares me. We're no' just fixin' a roof or mendin' a fence. We're buildin' somethin' that'll last. An' that thought—it makes me proud, aye. But it also keeps me awake at night."

Angus let out a dry chuckle. "Aye, I suppose we ought to get used tae that, eh?"

The three men shared a moment of silence, the fire crackling between them. It was rare for them to speak openly like this—rare, but necessary. Finally, Ewan smirked, taking a sip of his drink.

"Well, at least we've got each other tae suffer through it with. An' the women—though I daresay they'll handle all this better than we will."

Dougal laughed. "Aye, they'll be runnin' the place afore we ken it. We're just here tae do the heavy liftin'."

Angus grinned. "Then let's make sure we do it right. We've come too far tae let this place slip through our fingers."

Dougal raised his mug. "To Clachanoch, then. And to us."

Ewan and Angus followed suit, their drinks clinking together. The firelight danced in their eyes, and for all their worries, one truth settled among them—they had a long road ahead, but they would walk it together.

And somewhere deep within the bones of the house, the past listened—and approved.

THE EXPLORATION
CONTINUES

Despite having lived at Clachanoch Estate for several months, they had barely explored the vast basement area beneath the manor. Intrigued by the prospect of discovering hidden secrets, they gathered their lamps and descended into the dimly lit depths.

As they made their way through the basement, their footsteps echoing off the stone walls, they marvelled at the sheer size of the underground space. Dust-covered crates and forgotten relics lined the walls, hinting at the history that lay buried beneath the manor.

Dougal, Maree, Fiona, Angus, Ewan, and Morag moved cautiously, their lamps casting flickering shadows that danced across the walls. They came across a series of narrow corridors and hidden alcoves, each holding its own mystery and intrigue.

"It's like a maze down here," Angus remarked, his voice echoing through the cavernous space.

"Aye, but there's something exciting about it, dinnae ye think?" Dougal replied, his eyes shining with curiosity.

Fiona brushed her fingers along an old wooden barrel, sending a puff of dust into the air. "Imagine the folk who walked here afore us," she whispered. "Their footsteps... their stories. It's like they're still echoing."

Their exploration led them to a large, seemingly empty chamber at the far end of the basement. As they wandered through the chamber, Dougal noticed a peculiar pattern in the stonework near the far wall. Upon closer inspection, they discovered a small, almost imperceptible seam running along the floor.

"Could this be something?" Maree wondered aloud, her voice filled with excitement.

Dougal nodded, his heart pounding with anticipation. "Let's find out."

With a collective effort, they pushed against the seam, and to their amazement, a section of the floor slid aside, revealing a dark, narrow passageway leading into the depths below.

"By the saints, this must be a hidden chamber!" Angus exclaimed, his eyes wide with wonder.

Without hesitation, they ventured into the tunnel, their lamps casting a feeble light into the darkness ahead. The passage twisted and turned, leading them deeper into the earth, until finally, they emerged into a small, dusty chamber.

"Look at this," Fiona said, her voice barely above a whisper. "It's like somethin' out o' a storybook."

As they entered, their lamps revealed a sight that took their breath away. The chamber was filled with dusty old chests and crates, their contents obscured by years of neglect.

"What treasures do ye think lie within these chests?" Ewan mused, his eyes gleaming with excitement.

"Only one way ta find oot," Fiona said, stepping forward to inspect one of the chests.

As they carefully opened the chests, the group discovered a treasure trove of artefacts from Laird Graeme McBeth's era. In one chest, there were beautifully preserved garments made of rich fabrics, indicating the high status of the McBeth family. Fiona held up a velvet cloak, its deep blue hue still vibrant despite its age, marvelling at the intricate embroidery that adorned it.

Morag unwrapped a bundle of lace tucked beneath the garments. Nestled within was a child's bonnet, delicate and untouched by time. "It's so small," she murmured. "Was it meant for a McBeth bairn?"

Maree's voice was soft. "Or perhaps a bairn that never saw life. A memory wrapped in fabric."

The air grew still as they considered that possibility—a family's grief folded neatly away and buried with their legacy.

In another chest, they found stacks of yellowed parchment tied with faded ribbon. These turned out to be old letters and documents, detailing the daily affairs of the estate, as well as personal correspondence between Laird Graeme and other nobles of the time. The letters shed light on the political and social climate of the era, offering a glimpse into the life of the McBeth family.

Among the more curious discoveries were pieces of ancient weaponry. Swords, daggers, and even a few pieces of armour lay scattered among the chests, hinting at a time when Clachanoch Estate may have been embroiled in conflict. Each item was carefully examined, its craftsmanship admired, and its story imagined.

Dougal paused as he reached into one of the deeper crates and drew out a dagger, its handle wrapped in faded leather, the blade etched with runes.

"This... this belonged tae him. Laird Graeme," he whispered, his voice barely audible. A strange stillness settled over the group as they watched Dougal's expression shift—part wonder, part reverence. "It's like... I can feel him."

Nearby, Morag lifted a folded letter tied with ribbon, her hands trembling slightly as she read aloud. Her voice caught as she whispered the final line: "And if this ever reaches the hands of my kin... know that we fought to preserve this land, and all it stands for."

A quiet fell among them.

"They meant for us tae find this," Fiona murmured.

One small velvet case bore no jewellery—only a sealed envelope marked: "To the one who dares reclaim Clachanoch." They passed it around, hands gentle, before setting it aside to be read upstairs.

Having taken an inventory of the chests' contents, the group agreed that it would be best to bring them up to the manor for a more thorough examination. Dougal, in particular, was eager to study the maps and see if he could decipher where the other tunnels led.

"We've stumbled upon a treasure trove of history," Fiona said, her eyes shining with excitement. "Who knows what other secrets this estate holds?"

Morag spoke, "Let's take the chests upstairs intae the light so we can see everyt'ing clearly." Everyone agreed.

As the six of them carefully lifted the chests out of the secret hiding place, they carried them up into the manor and placed them on the dining room table. The room was bathed in the warm glow of the lamps, casting a soft light over the dusty old chests and the curious group surrounding them.

The very air in the room seemed to shift as they pried open the lids again. The silence wasn't empty—it was expectant. As if the walls themselves leaned in, waiting for the past to be spoken aloud.

With eager anticipation, they reopened the chests, revealing a trove of treasures inside. Among the items were several velvet-lined boxes, each containing exquisite necklaces, earrings, and other jewels. The gems sparkled in the light, casting shimmering reflections across the room.

"Would ye look at that," Angus exclaimed, his eyes wide with amazement.

"Aye, these are no ordinary trinkets," Dougal remarked, carefully examining a necklace. "These jewels are of significant value."

Fiona reached out to pick up one of the velvet boxes, her fingers trembling with excitement. "I wonder who tae belonged to? And why were tae hidden away like this?"

Maree gently opened one of the boxes, revealing a stunning necklace adorned with pearls and emeralds. "They must have belonged to someone of great importance," she said, her voice filled with awe.

Morag suddenly gasped, holding up a brooch shaped like a thistle entwined with a serpent. "I saw this same symbol in one o' the tapestry borders upstairs," she said. "It's a family crest, maybe?"

Dougal leaned in. "Aye... or a warning. The serpent entwined with the thistle—it could mean protectin' the land at any cost."

As they examined the jewels, they couldn't help but feel a sense of wonder at the history and mystery that surrounded them. These treasures were not just valuable in terms of their monetary worth, but also in the stories they held and the secrets they promised to reveal about Clachanoch Estate and its past. Yet, the chests held more than just riches—they held knowledge. Beneath the layers of jewels, Maree uncovered a bundle of old parchment, tied together with a frayed ribbon.

Carefully untying the ribbon, Maree spread the parchments across the table, revealing maps—intricate and detailed, showing the layout of the estate and the surrounding lands in great detail. The men, who had merely nodded politely at the jewels, suddenly leaned in with genuine interest. Dougal's eyes lit up as he studied them, tracing the winding paths of the tunnels and trying to match them to the landscape above.

"These tunnels seem to lead in all directions," Dougal said, his voice filled with excitement. "If we can decipher these maps, we might just find out where they all lead."

"Och, let the menfolk fuss ower their maps and tunnels," Fiona teased. "I'll be sittin' pretty draped in all these jewels!"

"Ye best hope that brooch disnae match yer fiery temper, Fiona, or ye'll set the whole estate alight!" Angus quipped, dodging the playful swat Fiona aimed at him.

As the laughter died down, Ewan leaned forward, his tone more serious. "D'ye think we ought tae report this? I mean... it's ours now, aye—but these artefacts, they're priceless. Somebody might come lookin'."

Dougal considered it. "We'll secure everythin' and document it proper. But for now, it stays in the family. We need time tae understand what we've found."

"Aye," Maree added, her gaze drifting back to the letter still sealed on the table. "Let's honour it right. Every piece has a story. And they chose us tae tell it."

Their discussion carried on into the evening, the group torn between their desire to honour the past and the need to ensure the treasures remained protected. Their talk of what to do with their discovery continued well into the next day, eventually weaving into their plans for the estate's future and the growing bond with the surrounding community.

Fiona stood later by the window, the sealed letter clutched in her hand. "Sometimes I wonder," she said, "if Clachanoch knew we were comin'. Like it waited for us."

Angus nodded. "Or maybe we were always meant tae come. Every step led us here."

She turned to him and smiled. "Then let's make it worth the wait."

Outside, the wind picked up, rattling the windows slightly. Fiona paused, glancing toward the darkened hallway. "It feels like we're bein' watched," she said softly, half-laughing, half-serious.

Dougal looked toward the hall, his hand brushing against the dagger once held by Laird Graeme. "Maybe we are," he said quietly. "But I think they're glad we're here."

And in that moment, surrounded by relics of the past and the people he trusted most, Dougal felt it too—a presence not threatening, but expectant. The past had found its voice.

And it had chosen them.

REKINDLING HOPE

As Clachanoch Estate began to flourish once again, the surrounding community warmed to the newcomers, appreciating their efforts to revitalise the land. The McBeth clan found themselves embraced by the villagers, who admired their hard work and determination.

One sunny afternoon, the village decided to organise a special meal to show their appreciation for the McBeths. Fiona, Morag, and Maree insisted on helping with the preparations, showcasing their culinary skills and warm hospitality. They visited the village shops, selecting the finest ingredients and sharing stories with the shopkeepers, who were eager to support the revitalisation of the estate.

"Good mornin', Mrs. MacGuigan," Fiona greeted warmly as they entered the butcher shop. "We'll need the finest cut o' lamb ye have. We're plannin' a feast."

"Ah, Fiona, it's wonderful tae see ye. The village is buzzin' aboot the meal. Here, take the best o' the lot," Mrs. MacGuigan replied, handing over a prime cut.

Next, they visited the grocers. "Mr. Fraser, we're lookin' for fresh herbs and vegetables. We want tae create somethin' truly special," Morag said, examining the produce.

"Ye ladies always have the best ideas," Mr. Fraser smiled. "Take whatever ye need. It's on the hoose."

As they passed the village green, children ran up to Maree, tugging at her hands and asking questions about Clachanoch. She knelt among them, her voice warm and inviting, weaving tales of the grand old halls and secret passageways. The bairns listened, wide-eyed, already dreaming of visiting one day.

The women took charge of the kitchen, working side by side with the villagers to prepare a feast fit for a king. Fiona's skill with herbs and spices added a tantalising aroma to the air.

"Fiona, what's yer secret with these herbs?" one of the villagers asked.

"Just a touch o' love and a lot o' patience," Fiona replied with a wink.

Morag's deft hands turned simple ingredients into mouth-watering dishes. "Morag, ye've outdone yerself with this stew," Maree commented, tasting a spoonful.

"Thank ye, Maree. It's the fresh produce from Mr. Fraser's shop. Makes all the difference," Morag responded, smiling.

Morag, with her quiet demeanour, ensured that everything ran smoothly, coordinating the cooking and serving with ease. "Let's make sure we have enough bread for everyone," she instructed. "And dinnae forget tae keep the cider flowin'."

That afternoon, Dougal and Ewan helped string up bunting made from old tartan scraps, fastening them between trees and doorposts. Angus rigged lanterns to hang from fence posts and over tables, muttering about ladders and his knees, but smiling all the same.

As the meal approached, the air was filled with excitement. Bairns ran around, helping to set up tables and decorate with wildflowers. The aroma of roasting meat and freshly baked bread filled the air, enticing everyone to gather around the long, communal tables.

During the meal, the community members and the Mc-Beths shared stories and laughter, forging bonds that would last a lifetime.

"Hard tae believe how much has changed since we first set foot here," Dougal remarked, raising his glass.

"Aye, and look at us now," Angus added. "We've made a good start, thanks tae everyone here."

Fiona and Morag's personalities shone through, their warmth and kindness leaving a lasting impression on everyone they met. "Yer cookin' is legendary, Fiona," one of the villagers praised.

"And yer hospitality, Morag. We're lucky tae have ye," another added.

Maree, with her fiery strength, became a pillar of support for the community, earning the respect and admiration of all. "Maree, yer organisational skills are unmatched," Ewan said, squeezing her hand.

Later in the evening, as musicians struck up a tune, Fiona grabbed Maree and spun her into a dance. Laughter pealed through the air as others joined, feet tapping on the packed earth. Even Angus gave a clumsy twirl before tripping over his own boots, sending the children into fits of giggles.

As the sun began to set, casting a warm glow over the gatherin', it was clear that the McBeths had found not just a place to call home, but a community that welcomed them with open arms. The meal symbolised the new beginning they had all worked so hard to achieve, a celebration of hope rekindled and a brighter future ahead.

As the last of the villagers drifted home and the night grew still, the McBeths gathered in the dining room of Clachanoch, mugs of cider in hand and firelight warming the walls. The table, once laden with food, now bore only candle stubs and crumbs—but their minds were full of the road ahead.

"Ye ken," Dougal began, glancing toward the cabinet where the velvet-lined boxes were safely tucked away, "we need tae talk about what we found. The jewels, the scrolls... all of it."

Angus grinned. "Aye, I say we build a grand museum an' charge admission—make ourselves a fortune."

Fiona scoffed. "Ye? Wi' yer dusty boots and grand plans? I'll believe it when I see it."

Laughter rang out, but the mood soon turned thoughtful.

"We cannae let it sit in boxes forever," Maree said. "There's history in those chests—lives, legacies. It's no' just treasure, it's truth."

"And the chapel," Morag added, softly. "It still calls tae me. Maybe the past is askin' us tae build somethin' again. Not just stone and mortar, but meaning."

Angus tapped the table. "Then maybe that's where we start. No' just with repairs, but with somethin' new—a centre for learning or remembrance. A place where people come to connect tae their roots."

They sat long into the night, weighing options, honouring memory, and imagining what might come next.

The next morning, as the warmth of the gathering still lingered, the men of Clachanoch Estate welcomed a group of local farmers to discuss revitalising the land. The idea of working together again, as in former times, seemed promising to both parties. A meeting was scheduled to walk the grounds and share ideas with Dougal, Angus, and Ewan.

On the appointed day, the farmers arrived, eager to see the estate's potential. Dougal, Angus, and Ewan led them on a tour of the grounds.

"Here's where we could plant the barley," Dougal suggested. "The soil's rich and should yield a good crop."

One of the older farmers knelt, running a handful of soil through his fingers. "Good earth," he muttered approvingly. "This land still has life in it."

"And we could raise livestock over there," Angus pointed. "There's plenty o' grazin' land."

As they walked, ideas flowed freely, with the farmers sharing their knowledge of the land and the best practices for farming in the area.

"I've had great success with crop rotation," one farmer mentioned. "It keeps the soil healthy."

"That's a brilliant idea," Ewan responded. "We could definitely implement that here."

After the tour, the group gathered in the dining room to further discuss their plans. The farmers were impressed by the estate's potential and expressed their willingness to work together to restore it to its former glory.

"We've got a lot o' work ahead of us, but I believe we can do it," Dougal said, his voice filled with determination.

"With everyone pullin' together, there's no doubt in my mind," Angus agreed.

As the meeting concluded, there was a sense of optimism in the air. The estate's partnership with the local farmers promised a bright future, not just for Clachanoch Estate but for the entire community. One farmer lingered behind, tapping the dusty floor with his cane. "It's good tae see life back in this place. My da worked here once...

it's been a long time since Clachanoch felt like home." He smiled at Dougal. "Now it does again."

CHAPTER 19

ELSPETH IN DREAMS

Dougal tossed and turned in his sleep, his dreams troubled by visions of a man standing in the turret, silhouetted against a dim and flickering light. This felt different—more vivid, more urgent. In his dream, Elspeth appeared, her voice soft but commanding, wrapped in the familiar calm that always seemed to steady him.

"Aye, Dougal, me lad," she said, her voice echoing as though carried on the wind. "Ye need tae look up there in that turret and see what mysteries lay there for ye. I'm comin', son. I'm comin'."

With a gasp, Dougal jolted upright, his heart pounding. Sweat clung to his brow despite the chill in the room. He sat in the silence, Elspeth's words clinging to him like fog.

He couldn't ignore the feeling in his gut—he had to look. Now.

He slipped from the bed, careful not to wake Maree, and grabbed a lamp from the dresser. The manor was silent as he crept through its winding halls and ascended the tight spiral staircase to the turret.

The air up there was still, untouched, heavy with dust. The stone walls glowed dull in the lamp's light. As he inspected the space, his hand grazed a slightly uneven stone. He paused. With careful fingers, he prodded it loose—and behind it, darkness.

A small cavity.

He reached in, his hand brushing something cold, smooth, and heavy. Heart hammering, he drew it out.

A gold bar.

He stared at it in disbelief. The thing gleamed even in the low light, its surface stamped with markings he didn't recognise. He reached in again and pulled out another.

"By the saints..." he whispered, stunned. "What on earth is this doin' here?" Dougal wondered aloud. But before he could ponder it further, another glint caught his eye. There was more! Dougal was beside himself with excitement. He carefully retrieved another gold bar from the hidden compartment.

Realising that gold bars were not something to be taken lightly, Dougal decided to take a couple downstairs. Although he hesitated, he gently woke Maree. She blinked sleepily, rubbing her eyes as she asked what was going on.

With a beaming smile, Dougal showed her the two gold bars he had retrieved from the turret.

Maree's eyes widened in astonishment as she examined the bars. "Dougal, where on earth did you find these?" she exclaimed, her voice filled with wonder.

"In the turret, lass! Can ye believe it?" Dougal replied, still in awe of his discovery. "There's more up there, I felt!"

Maree could hardly contain her excitement. "We must investigate further," she said, her mind racing with possibilities. "But not tonight. Let's get some rest and think about this in the morning."

With that, Dougal and Maree carefully stowed the gold bars away, their heads filled with visions of what other treasures might lie hidden within the ancient walls of Clachanoch Estate.

Even as Maree drifted back to sleep, Dougal sat upright beside her, staring at the darkened ceiling, pulse still racing. It wasn't just about the gold. It was about the message Elspeth had left him—the whisper of a legacy still unfolding.

Before dawn, while the rest of the house lay in peaceful slumber, Dougal couldn't resist revisiting the turret. He returned alone, lifting out three more gold bars and a small, sealed box wrapped in linen. The box was heavier than expected. Curious but cautious, he brought it downstairs and tucked it away in the locked drawer of the old sideboard.

The next morning, after breakfast, Dougal gathered everyone around. "Right, everyone, we've got somethin' to show ye," he announced. Maree placed the gold bars gently on the table.

"Last night, Dougal found these," she said. "And this morning, he brought down more."

The group gasped as the bars caught the sunlight. Fiona leaned closer. "This is... incredible. But who hid it—and why?"

"That's the mystery, lass," Dougal replied. "And it's no' the only one. Some nights ago, when I was havin' a wee dram with the men, talkin' and things, I was lookin' into the flames. I had a vision of a man in the turret. Then Elspeth appeared in a dream, tellin' me to look up there."

Dougal recounted the dream, Elspeth's voice echoing through his mind. The mention of her made them all pause.

"And she said, 'I'm comin', son,'" Dougal added quietly.

Angus rubbed his jaw. "That's no ordinary dream. Ye're being guided."

"Ye really think Elspeth led ye to it?" Angus asked, more sceptical than the rest.

"Aye," Fiona said. "She's done stranger things."

"What do ye think it all means?" Angus asked, his curiosity piqued.

"I'm no' sure, but I think there's more tae discover in this estate than we ever imagined," Dougal said, his eyes shining with excitement. "And I reckon we're just gettin' started."

As the group discussed the implications of the discovery, Maree suggested they explore the turret further to see if there were more hidden treasures. Excitement filled the air as they made their way up to the turret, eager to unravel the mystery.

After a careful search, more gold bars were unearthed—along with old coins, and tucked behind a final stone, a velvet pouch.

Inside was a folded note.

Dougal opened it with trembling hands:

To those who find this,

This gold was hidden in a time of great financial increase. If you are reading this, then the estate has likely passed through darkness and hardship. These resources are not for greed but for restoration. Use them to rebuild what was lost. Honour the name of McBeth.

—Laird Alasdair McBeth

A long silence followed.

"He left it... for us," Maree said softly.

"It's ours now," Dougal added. "But we keep it quiet. Just for us, for now."

"Aye," said Ewan. "It could stir the wrong kind of attention."

"We'll use it wisely," Morag said. "As it was meant to be."

As they examined the treasures, Dougal couldn't shake the feeling that there was more to uncover. "I think there's still more secrets to this place," he said, his voice echoing with determination. "We need to keep exploring, keep digging, until we uncover the truth of Clachanoch Estate."

Fiona, still turning the velvet pouch over in her hand, murmured, "What if there's more than gold? What if there's knowledge... ancient, dangerous even? We should be careful, aye?" The others fell into thoughtful silence, the weight of her words settling over them like dusk.

As they descended, they found the parlour unusually quiet. A soft knock at the door startled them. Dougal opened it—and there stood Elspeth.

Only... she had not knocked.

"Elspeth!" Maree greeted her with warmth. "Ye always arrive at the right time."

"Do I?" Elspeth smiled. "Funny that."

Fiona grinned. "Come in. We've a tale to share."

Elspeth walked in slowly, eyes taking in the room. Her gaze settled on Dougal.

"I told ye the land speaks, Dougal," she said. "And it listens too."

She leaned close and gently tapped his chest.

"But most of all, it listens to this."

He blinked, moved but unsure.

"You've the sight, lad. Same as me. Don't question it. Trust it."

Maree touched Elspeth's arm. "Did ye really visit him in a dream?"

Elspeth only smiled. "What's a dream but a door, lass? And some o' us ken how to walk through."

Before she turned to leave, she added, "Check the old study. There's a ledger ye've overlooked. In the drawer, bottom left."

Then, without another word, she vanished into the mist beyond the door. Angus watched her go, rubbing his neck.

"I'll never get used tae that."

Later, in the study, they found it—an old ledger exactly where Elspeth had said. Inside, detailed accounts, dated and signed by Laird Alasdair, documenting how the estate had once functioned efficiently, responsibly, with profits and provisions.

And in the back—a folded appendix.

Maree unfolded it slowly:

Clause 17 — The Heir's Provision: Should the estate fall into disrepair, and an heir restore it with clear evidence of moral and financial stewardship, then access to the McBeth Provision shall be granted.

Below that line was a second in a different hand.

Provision secured. Turret. Other places to be advised.

They stared at it, hearts pounding.

"We've fulfilled it," Dougal said. "He knew we'd come. He prepared for it."

Fiona wiped a tear from her cheek. "Elspeth knew too."

As the fire crackled in the grate, they sat in a reverent hush. The estate was no longer a mystery they were solving—it was a calling they were answering.

And with gold in their hands, Elspeth's guidance at their backs, and Clachanoch's legacy rising before them—they were ready for what lay ahead.

Dougal reached over and gripped Angus's shoulder. "We need tae draw up plans. Restore the chapel. Invest in the land. Maybe start a school. Let the estate serve more than just us." Angus nodded slowly, and a flicker of pride glinted in his eyes.

Then suddenly Maree looked at them all, "Aye, ye a bit premature! What's dis 'other places to be advised' mean? Does it mean, there's moor to be found?"

Dougal looked at his wife, "Lass, you're right. There's more to be found. But fir noo, let's be thankful for what we have noo."

BREAKING THE CHAINS

The evening was still, save for the occasional whisper of wind rattling the ancient glass panes of Clachanoch. The manor had always been full of voices—echoes of the past murmuring through its stone corridors, waiting to be acknowledged.

Dougal sat alone in the study, a dram of whisky untouched in his hand, staring at the flickering candlelight. The gold bars had been carefully stored away, their discovery still fresh in his mind, but it was not the fortune that weighed on him. It was something deeper. Something restless inside him.

Elspeth's words echoed in his mind: Ye've always had the sight, Dougal, me lad... trust in yer instincts. It was a truth he had long ignored, yet the more he fought against it, the stronger it pulled him toward something inevitable.

He reached for the old documents they had uncovered, fingers tracing the aged parchment. The names of his ancestors stared back at him, some familiar, others unknown. They had all carried burdens of their own—dreams, failures, expectations. Was he simply another link in a never-ending chain of men trying to prove their worth?

A sound from the hallway startled him. Not a creak or groan, but a whisper. Faint, indistinct—like his name being carried on a breeze. He rose slowly, leaving the whisky behind, and stepped into the corridor. The shadows seemed deeper than usual, and the lanterns flickered as if disturbed by something unseen.

The door creaked open slightly, and Maree stepped inside, her keen gaze catching the storm of thoughts that played across his face.

"Ye're broodin' again," she said lightly, moving to sit across from him. "That head of yers does too much thinkin' for one man."

Dougal exhaled, rubbing his temples. "It's this place, Maree. It's as if the past willnae rest until it's been made right. I keep feelin' like I'm bein' pulled toward somethin', somethin' that's been buried too long."

Maree leaned forward, her voice softer now. "Maybe ye're meant tae find it. Or maybe it's been findin' you all along."

Dougal looked at her then, something shifting in his expression. He reached for her hand, grounding himself in her steady warmth. "There's a reckoning comin'," he admitted. "And I dinnae think it's just about this estate. It's about me."

Maree squeezed his hand. "Then face it, Dougal. But dinnae carry it alone."

The words settled deep within him, pressing against something raw and unspoken. He nodded, though the weight in his chest had not lifted. Not yet.

The night stretched on, the candle burning low. Eventually, when Dougal closed his eyes, he knew the past was not finished with him.

And in the depths of his dreams – or was it reality, the cliffs of his childhood rose up before him—waiting.

As Dougal stood on the cliff's edge, facing the ghostly image of his father, Tally McBeth, he felt a surge of emotion unlike anything he'd experienced before. The wind howled around him, echoing the turmoil within his heart.

"Why, Faither?" Dougal's voice was raw with emotion, his words carrying the weight of years of pain and anguish. "Why were ye sae harsh, sae distant? Why could ye never see me for who I am?"

Tally's spectral form remained stoic, unmoved by Dougal's outburst.

"I expected greatness frae ye, Dougal," Tally's voice was cold, cutting. "But ye always fell short. Ye were never enough."

Dougal's anger flared, his frustration boiling over. "Was it worth it, Faither? Worth pushin' me away, makin' me feel like I was never good enough? What did ye gain frae it?"

His voice rose to a yell, echoing off the cliffs. "Answer me, damn ye! Why did ye have tae be sae cruel?"

A sudden gust tore through the vision, forcing Dougal back a step. For a moment, he thought the cliff itself had cracked open beneath him—but no, it was just the force of memory. His jaw clenched with tension, but then he spoke again, a bit quieter now.

A memory flashed—Dougal as a bairn, barely ten, dropping a heavy sack of feed on the croft. Tally's voice barking, "Ye're weak, boy! Weak and soft, just like yer mother's kin." The sting of shame, of being dismissed, had never truly faded.

Tally's ghostly form flickered, a hint of regret passing over his features. "I was a fool, Dougal. A fool who could never measure up tae the standards placed upon me by my ain faither," he began, his voice filled with remorse. "He constantly bemoaned that he wished he was able tae go back and claim Clachanoch Estate for himself, tae right what he saw as a great injustice. I thought that by bein' harsh wi' ye, I could somehow make up for my ain failings, my ain failed dreams."

Tally paused, the weight of his words hanging heavy in the air. "My faither pushed upon me the idea that I should try also tae reclaim the estate, which I flat out refused. This caused further friction between us, as he couldnae understand why I would nae pursue what he saw as our birthright. But I could nae bring myself tae follow in his footsteps, tae live a life driven by the pursuit of land and power. I wanted something different for myself, something more."

Dougal listened intently, his anger softening as he began to understand the complexities of his father's past. He realised that Tally was burdened by his own father's expectations, just as he had been burdened by Tally's. The cycle of pain and regret stretched back through generations, each father passing on his own unfulfilled dreams and desires to his son.

"It ends with me," Dougal whispered, the wind tugging at his coat. "I willnae pass this on. No more boys growin' up feelin' small in their faither's shadow." His voice rang with quiet conviction, a vow made not just to Tally, but to himself.

Dougal's anger softened, replaced by a deep sadness. "Faither, why didn't ye ever tell me this? Why didn't ye share yer pain wi' me?"

Tally's form began to shimmer, his voice growing emotional. "I was a proud man, Dougal. Too proud tae admit my ain shortcomings, my ain failures. But I see now that I was wrong. I see the pain I caused ye, and I'm sorry."

But Dougal was not done. Years of pent-up emotion poured out of him, a torrent of anger and hurt. "Sorry? Sorry isn't enough, Faither! Ye ruined me, made me feel like I was nuthin'! I'll never be able tae forget what ye did tae me!"

Tally's ghostly form began to flicker, on the verge of disappearing. "I know, Dougal. I know. But ye have a chance tae be better, tae break the cycle. Forgive me, son. Be better than me, son. Let that be enough."

Standing on the cliff's edge, watching his father's ghost disappear into the wind, Dougal felt a mix of emotions swirling inside him. Anger, sadness, regret—all of it threatened to overwhelm him. But as he took a deep breath, he felt a sense of calm wash over him.

"I forgive ye, Faither," he whispered into the wind. "I forgive ye for everything."

With those words, a weight lifted from Dougal's shoulders, a burden he had carried for far too long. He turned away from the cliff and began the long walk home, each step lighter than the last.

"I may never be what ye wanted me tae be," he said to himself, his voice firm and resolute. "But I am who I am, and that's enough."

As he turned away from the cliffs, the first light of dawn crested the horizon, painting the sky in hues of gold and crimson. Dougal inhaled deeply, the crisp air filling his lungs.

He was ready to move forward.

To lead Clachanoch.

To forge his own path—not out of obligation, but out of choice.

And for the first time in his life, he truly felt free.

Dougal made his way home. The manor stood ahead, solid and waiting, just as it always had. His boots were heavy with the weight of the night's journey, but his heart—his heart felt lighter.

Maree was already awake, standing at the doorway as though she had known he would return now. She studied his face, reading the exhaustion in his eyes, but also something else—something new.

Without a word, she stepped forward, wrapping her arms around him. Dougal exhaled, resting his forehead against her shoulder, letting her warmth anchor him.

"Ye found what ye needed?" she asked softly.

"Aye," Dougal murmured. "And I let it go."

Maree pulled back slightly, her hands resting on either side of his face. "Good, my love. Now come inside. Yer home."

And with that, Dougal stepped over the threshold, leaving the ghosts of the past behind.

TO THE MANOR BORN

As Clachanoch Estate continued its journey of renewal, the group of six found themselves faced with the task of repairing the roof and restoring the upper servants' rooms. The discovery of the hidden gold bars provided them with the means to fund these much-needed repairs.

Dougal, Angus, and Ewan set out to exchange some of the gold bars for cash, ensuring they had enough to cover the cost of materials and labour. Meanwhile, Fiona, Maree, and Morag focused on the interior restoration, breathing new life into the manor's once-grand rooms.

Each morning began with the scent of peat smoke and the sound of hammering echoing through the glen. The men rose early to lift slates, replace rotten beams, and patch chimney stacks, while the women lit fires to chase off the damp and flung open windows to let in the sharp Highland air. Meals were shared outside when weather allowed, seated on barrels or stone steps, laughter rising with the steam from tin mugs of tea. It was hard, honest work—the kind that blisters the hands and binds hearts together.

The women worked tirelessly, cleaning and repairing the damaged areas, carefully preserving the estate's history and character. Fiona took charge of overseeing the repairs, her keen eye for detail ensuring that every room was restored to its former glory. Maree's artistic flair added a touch of elegance to the decor, while Morag's practical skills proved invaluable in tackling the more challenging tasks.

As the repairs progressed, the manor began to regain its former splendour. The roof was repaired, the upper servants' rooms were restored, and the interior was transformed into a warm and inviting space. The community watched in awe as Clachanoch Estate underwent its remarkable transformation, a testament to the group's hard work and dedication.

Fiona, being of middle age and well-travelled, took charge of decorating some of the fifteen bedrooms that dotted the manor. Drawing from her experiences in the Middle East, Asia, and the islands, she adorned the rooms with an eclectic mix of artefacts and unusual objects she had collected throughout the years. To add warmth and luxury, Fiona hung thick, lined fabric on the walls, creating a cosy ambience. She chose a colour palette of lilac, gold, burgundy, and silver, which complemented the rich textures and patterns of the fabrics.

Ensuring comfort was paramount, Fiona personally attended to the mattresses, restuffing them and adding springs for extra support. Large bed frames were restored to their former glory, with hanging curtains and bed canopies adding a touch of elegance. The windows were not overlooked; Fiona installed triple-thickness curtains that not only hung beautifully but also helped to keep the warmth in during the colder months.

Some rooms were a collaborative effort, with all the women coming together to share stories and laughter as they worked. The end result was a collection of bedrooms that exuded charm, comfort, and a hint of exotic allure, a true reflection of Fiona's unique style and the women's collective vision.

Morag, with her village-girl charm and practical nature, set about transforming the twenty odd servants' rooms into havens of semi-luxury and comfort, without tipping into extravagance. She envisioned metal double beds for future visitors and two single beds for siblings or other guests. The colour palette she chose was a soothing blend of blues, greens, cream, and touches of gold, creating a simple yet elegant ambience.

Maree's vision for the kitchen was both practical and charming. She wanted a large, sturdy table at the centre, perfect for both dining and food preparation, reminiscent of a rustic French provincial kitchen. Pots and pans were to be hung from hooks on the ceiling, adding a practical touch and giving the kitchen a cosy, lived-in feel. The simple chandeliers she chose added a touch of elegance without being overly ostentatious.

As Maree sang a wee Scottish song to herself, lost in her thoughts while cleaning the fireplace, she noticed something peculiar. A crack in the stones seemed to be absorbing a lot of the water she was using. Curiosity piqued, she set aside her cleaning implements and began to trace the stones with her hands. To her shock, one of the stones moved slightly. Intrigued, she managed to wriggle the stone loose, revealing a hidden compartment behind it.

With her lamp casting a flickering light into the dark recesses of the fireplace, Maree's eyes widened in amazement. Bars of gold and silver were stacked neatly inside, disappearing behind another stone. She couldn't contain her excitement and let out a squeal of delight. Without hesitation, she ran up to the roof, calling for Dougal.

"Dougal, me love, ye'll want tae come and see what I've discover'ed in the kitchen fireplace. Come down now, will ye?"

Dougal, intrigued by Maree's excitement, hurried down to the kitchen. As he approached, he could see the gleam of precious metals in the fireplace. He was astonished.

"How did ye find this, Maree?" he asked, his eyes wide with wonder.

Maree beamed with pride. "I was just cleanin' the fireplace, and I noticed a stone that seemed out of place. When I moved it, I found all this!"

Together, they carefully removed the bars of gold and silver from the hidden compartment. It was a moment of pure joy and disbelief.

Dougal gathered the group around the table, the glow of the lamp casting a warm light on their eager faces. "With the repairs already taken care of, we have a unique opportunity to use this new cache of gold bars to not only sustain the estate but to truly revitalise it," he began, his voice filled with excitement.

That night, before sleep overtook them, the six gathered in the sitting room beside the fire. Ewan passed around glasses of peaty whisky, and they toasted to the unknown hands who'd hidden the treasure, to the legacy they were restoring, and to the unlikely friendship that had grown between them. For a long while, no one spoke—there was no need. The crackle of the fire and the ticking of the long-case clock spoke volumes.

After the excitement of the newest find, the women led their men up to the rooms they had spent months cleaning, restoring, and redecorating. The men were suitably impressed, marvelling at the transformation of the once-dusty and neglected rooms into elegant and inviting spaces.

Ewan, gazing around one of the newly finished rooms, remarked softly, "Never thought I'd see a night like this." His voice was tinged with quiet wonder.

Feeling a sense of gratitude and wanting to do something special for the women, the men decided to take them down to the local pub for an early dinner. They knew it was a rare treat for the women to be allowed in, but they were determined to make the evening memorable.

The pub was alive with energy, the scent of roasted meats and fresh ale mingling in the air. Laughter filled the space as locals greeted the group with friendly nods, acknowledging their efforts in restoring Clachanoch Estate. The barkeep, a stout man with a twinkle in his eye, greeted them heartily. "Ah, the McBeths and their fine company! Come in, come in! A round on the house, in honour of yer hard work!"

Beside him stood his wife, a sprightly woman with silver-streaked hair and a knowing smile. "It's no' every day we see women in here, and never with so much class. Sit yerselves down—we've saved ye the big table."

The group settled at a large wooden table, drinks in hand, the warmth of the fire seeping into their bones. Morag and Fiona exchanged glances, both amused at the novelty of being inside the village pub.

"Feels strange, does it not?" Morag murmured, eyeing the crowd. "Like we've stepped into a man's world."

Fiona chuckled. "Aye, but I dare say they'll be used to us soon enough."

Just then, a familiar face approached—Elspeth, wrapped in a tartan shawl, holding a bouquet of wild thistle and heather. "For the lasses," she said, smiling as she placed them in front of Fiona. "Clachanoch doesnae just need walls restored. It needs heart. And that's what you've all brought back." The gesture brought mist to more than one pair of eyes.

The evening carried on in good spirits, the music swelling as a fiddler began to play. Encouraged by the rhythm, Dougal stood and extended a hand to Maree. "Come on, lass, let's give them somethin' to talk about."

Maree laughed, setting down her drink and taking his hand. They moved across the floor, spinning and stepping to the lively reel. Soon, Angus and Fiona joined in, followed by Morag and Ewan, until they were all caught up in the joyous dance. The locals clapped along, some cheering, others joining the fun, turning the night into a full-blown celebration.

When they finally collapsed back into their seats, breathless and exhilarated, the barkeep brought over another round. "If I didnae know better, I'd say ye lot were born for this place."

Dougal raised his glass, meeting the eyes of each of his friends. "Maybe we were." And with that, they toasted to their home, their future, and the legacy they were building—together.

THE UNEXPECTED
ENCOUNTER

The evening had settled into a quiet hum at Clachanoch Estate, the flickering fire casting dancing shadows across the walls. The dining room table was strewn with their discoveries—maps, letters, jewels—bathed in the amber glow of the lamps. Dougal, Maree, Fiona, Angus, Ewan, and Morag sat deep in discussion, their voices weaving together like the threads of history they were slowly unravelling.

Dougal ran his fingers over the ancient map before him, tracing the delicate inked lines. His mind churned with possibilities—hidden passages, long-forgotten secrets. There had always been an unspoken connection between him and this land, but tonight, that connection felt more tangible than ever. As though the very stones of Clachanoch were whispering to him.

Outside, the wind shifted direction, brushing past the windows with a low sigh, as though something unseen were moving through the night. In the distance, the hoot of an owl rang clear, followed by the rustle of branches. The estate held its breath, as if bracing for what was about to unfold.

A sudden chill settled over the room. It was subtle, like a draft slipping through the cracks, but it carried an energy that made the hairs on his arms stand on end. The firelight flickered strangely, casting elongated shadows that stretched unnaturally along the walls. A faint hum—low, resonant—seemed to seep from the manor itself.

Dougal stilled.

The air thickened, charged with something unseen, something ancient.

And then—he was no longer alone.

A figure emerged from the dimness, not stepping into the light so much as forming from it. He was tall, his presence commanding, with the regal bearing of a leader and the weight of centuries in his piercing gaze. His clothing, though spectral, bore the fine detail of a warrior's cloak, a chieftain's crest, the unmistakable air of nobility.

Dougal's breath hitched. The others remained absorbed in their studies, oblivious to the apparition standing before him.

"Who... who are ye?" Dougal's voice barely carried, caught between awe and trepidation.

The man regarded him with an expression both knowing and measured. "I am the Mormaer of Moray," he intoned, his voice deep, threaded with the echoes of a hundred battles. "And ye, Dougal McBeth, have awakened the legacy of my land."

Dougal's pulse thundered in his ears. The Mormaer. A title of ancient power, of warriors and rulers who had fought for the Highlands before Scotland was even a name. And now, here he stood, bound not by flesh but by something older, something bound to the land itself.

A golden glow began to pulse faintly beneath the table, illuminating the underside of the map. It wasn't firelight—this light shimmered with a soft radiance, alive, almost breathing. The runes on the edges of the parchment began to shine faintly, responding to the presence of the Mormaer as though recognising their master.

"Ye have uncovered much," the Mormaer continued, his gaze sweeping over the table where the relics of Clachanoch lay. "But there is more. The tunnels beneath this estate are not merely passageways. They are the veins of the land—leading tae the heart of its power, its secrets."

Dougal swallowed hard, his throat dry. "What lies in these tunnels?"

The Mormaer lifted a hand, and the very walls of the room seemed to tremble in response. Faint, ancient runes shimmered across the stones, symbols Dougal did not recognise yet felt in his very bones.

"Deep within," the Mormaer said, "lies knowledge preserved through the ages. Writings of the ancient ones, the first keepers of this land—those who understood its rhythms, its elements, its power. Their wisdom has remained hidden, protected, waiting for those who would honour it. But only those with pure hearts and true intent will be permitted tae claim it."

A rush of possibilities flooded Dougal's mind. The land's history was already vast, but this... this was something beyond treasure, beyond wealth. This was knowledge. Power. A legacy hidden beneath their feet.

"But why now? Why show yerself tae me?" Dougal asked, his voice steadier now.

The Mormaer's expression softened, his presence shifting from formidable to something near fatherly. "Because the time has come," he said simply. "Ye and yer kin—ye are the guardians now. The land has chosen ye, just as it once chose me. But ken this, Dougal McBeth—knowledge is no' given freely. It must be earned.

The wise woman who walks between the veils... her footsteps echo still. Ye've felt her hand on yer path."

From somewhere within the house, a clock began to chime—not the grand hall one, but a small mantelpiece timepiece in a far-off room, as if echoing through dimensions. The Mormaer's eyes flicked in its direction, and for a moment, a flicker of sadness crossed his expression. Time, it seemed, was still very much part of the bargain.

A vision flashed before Dougal's eyes—a battlefield drenched in mist, warriors clashing, the weight of blood and sacrifice heavy in the air. Then, just as swiftly, the vision shifted—quiet halls of learning, hands tracing ancient symbols, the hushed reverence of a sacred duty. He felt the land's heartbeat beneath his feet, pulsing in time with his own.

His destiny had been woven into Clachanoch's fabric long before he had ever set foot upon it.

"What ye seek lies beyond the circle not of stone... but of soul."

"Where dae we start?" Dougal asked, resolve solidifying in his chest.

The Mormaer nodded approvingly. "The tunnels will guide ye, but the true path is not one of stone alone—it is one of spirit. The guardians of this place will not yield their wisdom lightly. Approach with respect, and only then will they reveal what has been kept hidden. The tunnels once ran with more than water. The land has not forgotten. Ye will need its forgiveness, before ye walk freely."

The glow around the Mormaer began to fade, his form dissolving into shadow, but his final words lingered in the air like an oath.

"The path is yours now, Dougal McBeth. Guard it well."

And then he was gone.

The fire crackled. The room stilled. The air, though warmer, still hummed with something unseen.

Dougal remained frozen in place, the weight of the encounter pressing upon him. He exhaled, long and slow, before glancing around at his wife and friends. They were still pouring over their findings, oblivious to what had just transpired.

His hands clenched into fists. He needed to tell them.

"Everyone," he called, his voice steady, yet carrying an urgency they did not miss. As they turned toward him, he took a breath, feeling the magnitude of the words he was about to speak.

"We have a new quest before us. The tunnels beneath Clachanoch lead tae something much greater than we imagined. The writings of the first keepers—the secrets of the Mormaer—they're real. And they are waitin' for us."

Maree frowned slightly, but intrigue flickered in her eyes. "How dae ye ken this?"

Angus, who had once scoffed at tales of spirits and ancient energies, now found himself strangely silent. Something about Dougal's face—his pallor, the weight in his eyes—made her spine prickle. Whatever had happened, it had shaken him to his very core.

"Because I was just told," Dougal answered simply, his gaze unwavering. "By the Mormaer himself."

A hush fell over the room.

Fiona, ever the believer, arched an eyebrow. "Ye're serious, then? Ye saw him?"

"Aye," Dougal nodded. "And he told me what we must do. These tunnels are no' just passageways—they are protected. If we want tae uncover their secrets, we must prove ourselves worthy."

Maree, watching him closely, touched his arm. "Ye're white as a ghost, Dougal. Sit down a moment."

He obeyed, quietly grateful for the steadiness of her touch.

Angus exhaled, rubbing the back of his neck. "Well, that does complicate things a wee bit, doesn't it?"

Morag, on the other hand, looked positively alight with excitement. "Then what are we waitin' for?" she grinned. "If we're tae be the guardians of this place, let's get tae work!"

Dougal's lips quirked into a small smile. Aye, this was his clan. His family. The ones who would stand beside him, no matter the task ahead.

He reached for the map, his fingers once more tracing the hidden tunnels.

The journey into the heart and soul of Clachanoch had only just begun.

"Guard it well," Dougal murmured, the Mormaer's words still echoing in his heart.

THE HIDDEN LEGACY

Energised by the discovery and the Mormaer's revelation, the group quickly realised that the chests and jewels were just the beginning. The real mystery lay deeper within the tunnels, where the true secrets of Clachanoch were hidden. With a renewed sense of purpose, Dougal, Maree, Fiona, Angus, Ewan, and Morag ventured back into the passageway, their lanterns casting flickering shadows along the ancient stone walls.

The sound of their footsteps echoed off the stone with a rhythm that felt almost ceremonial, as though the passage itself acknowledged their return. Dust hung in the air like a veil, disturbed only by the golden sway of their lamplight, revealing cobwebs spun like lace across corners and alcoves. Every creak of wood or groan of stone sent a ripple of tension through the group—but not fear. Anticipation.

The air grew colder and damper as they descended, the narrow passageways twisting and turning, as if designed to confuse an intruder. The deeper they went, the more they saw signs that this place was not merely a hiding place, but something more.

"Look at thaese symbols," Fiona whispered, running her fingers over the carvings. "They be tellin' a story. This isn't just a tunnel—it's a record."

Dougal nodded, studying the etchings. "This must be frae the time o' the Mormaer of Moray. He and his people built these for a reason."

And then, something shifted in their understanding.

These tunnels were not simply an escape route. They were a fortress beneath the land. A defensive network meant to protect the people in times of war, a place of last refuge when their enemies came. The Mormaer's people had carved out their survival here—not just through brute strength but through strategy. The hidden caches of weapons, supplies, and treasures were not just relics. They were preparations. A safeguard against annihilation.

The deeper they delved, the more the air seemed charged with the weight of history.

Maree paused as they turned a corner, her hand lightly brushing the tunnel wall. "It feels like they never left," she murmured. "Like their spirits are still here, waitin' for someone tae carry it on." The others slowed too, struck by the same eerie sense of presence. The silence pressed in—not menacing, but solemn. As if the very stone remembered those who once walked here with sword in hand and hope in their hearts.

After what felt like hours of navigating the twisting passages, they came upon a massive arched doorway—an iron-bound gate, reinforced with thick wooden beams. It had not simply been built; it had been fortified.

Dougal ran his hands over the structure. "This was meant tae withstand a siege."

Carved into the stone were battle scenes—clashes between warriors, ships arriving from the north, fortifications standing strong against invaders. The Mormaer had spoken of the conflicts between the Scottish and Norse forces. Perhaps this was their last stand—a place where knowledge and people could be preserved if the land above was lost.

With a concerted effort, they pushed the doors open.

What they saw beyond took their breath away.

The chamber was vast—a war room of sorts, lined with stone pillars, its walls etched with maps of the region. At the centre stood a great wooden table, where battle strategies, hidden routes, and records of alliances had once been planned. But most astonishing was the library of scrolls and records—an archive of history meant to preserve knowledge that the world above would one day forget.

A hush fell over them, as though even their breathing might disturb something sacred. Fiona stepped back instinctively, eyes wide with reverence. "This is more than a stronghold," she whispered. "It's a covenant. They meant this tae last beyond their own lifetimes." The weight of that truth settled over them all. They were not intruders here. They were the inheritors.

Maree stepped forward, her voice hushed in reverence. "This is nae just a treasure room... it's a command centre."

Dougal carefully picked up one of the old scrolls and unrolled it, his breath catching as he read. These were not spells, nor mystical incantations—these were accounts of battle tactics, treaties, and coded messages meant to outwit the enemy. Another scroll spoke of diplomacy: careful negotiations made in secret between Highland clans. Still others contained agricultural practices, seasonal guides, and even herbal medicine recipes—designed to keep the community self-sufficient.

"These tunnels... this place..." Fiona murmured, scanning the shelves. "It was meant tae be a sanctuary. If tae Mormaer fell in battle, this was where hes people wo'ld regroup, where they'd make dae last stand."

Ewan exhaled sharply, realisation dawning. "They built all this tae survive. This was never about hoardin' power—it was about preservin' their people, their knowledge, their way of life."

Morag stepped forward, her brow furrowed in concentration as she examined a scroll carefully rolled and sealed in wax. "This one looks different—like it's personal. Aye, it's written in a woman's hand," she murmured. "Could be a healer, or a leader in her own right."

Angus ran a hand through his hair, letting out a low whistle. "We're sittin' on one o' the most important pieces o' history Scotland's ever seen, and no one even kens it's here."

Fiona's mind was already racing. "This changes everythin'. If we can piece these records together, we canna rewrite history—show da world what really happened durin' the wars."

But Dougal wasn't thinking of history books. He was thinking of the present—the land they now called home.

His gaze settled on a map, nearly as long as the table, carefully preserved beneath a sheet of hardened wax. As he examined it, something caught his eye—a series of underground routes leading far beyond Clachanoch Estate.

"We be wrong," he said slowly. "These tunnels... thae don't just protect Clachanoch." He pointed at the lines stretching across the map. "They connect to other strongholds. Other hidden places."

Morag leaned in, eyes widening. "Ye mean tae say... there are more?"

"Aye." Dougal's heart pounded. "This is just one piece of a much larger puzzle."

This wasn't about magic or mysticism.

It was about a network of resistance—an entire system of fortifications built to defend Scotland from invaders.

And they had just stumbled upon one of its last remaining secrets.

The torchlight flickered across the carved stonework above the far arch, and for a fleeting moment, Maree thought she saw movement—like the shadow of someone watching, then gone. She blinked, uncertain. But when she turned to Dougal, his gaze was already there, fixed on the same spot. Neither spoke of it, but both felt it: the past wasn't dead. It was alive, and listening.

Maree set her hands on the table, steadying herself. "If dat's true... then we have tae protect this place."

Dougal nodded. "Aye. And if there are others out there, we need tae find them."

On the far wall, Fiona noticed something she hadn't before—a carved crest with a spiralling symbol woven into a Celtic knot. Below it were the words etched in old Gaelic: "To remember, to resist, to restore."

"That's the mark," she breathed. "It's a sigil. If we see this again... we'll ken we've found another."

They stood in silent awe.

Their mission was no longer just about restoring Clachanoch.

They were now the keepers of a history that had nearly been erased.

And as they carefully gathered the most fragile scrolls, preparing to return to the surface, they knew one thing for certain:

In an instant, everything they thought they knew had changed—and the legacy of the Mormaer was only beginning to reveal itself.

THE CHOSEN GUARDIAN

The group emerged from the depths of the tunnels, the weight of the scrolls heavy in their arms. Though exhilaration buzzed just beneath the surface, Dougal couldn't shake the unease tightening in his chest. The Mormaer's revelation had changed everything. Clachanoch was no longer simply their home—it was a sacred trust, a legacy, and he had been chosen to bear its weight.

As they crossed the threshold into the manor, the flickering lanterns cast long shadows down the stone hallways, and Dougal lingered behind, his thoughts churning. He could almost feel the heartbeat of the estate beneath his feet, steady and ancient. What had once been a crumbling inheritance now pulsed with a sense of living purpose. His father's voice echoed faintly in his memory, sharp and disapproving, but also layered with things unsaid. Dougal paused, running his hand along the stone wall, and whispered, "I hope ye're watchin' now."

As he stood alone for a breath longer, a strange warmth settled in his chest—not unlike the feeling he'd known as a lad when tales of knights, rebels, and hidden realms had filled his head. Back then, it was books and fireside stories that painted his world with wonder. Now, standing within these ancient walls, it felt as if those boyhood imaginings had been more prophecy than play. The whispers of the land, once distant dreams, were now pressing close—real, rooted, and waiting.

After securing the scrolls in a locked cabinet deep within the study, the group gathered in the grand hall. The fire crackled in the hearth, casting flickering shadows along the stone walls, as though the very foundation of Clachanoch held its breath. Dougal stood at the head of the long wooden table, hands braced against it. Despite the turmoil inside him, his voice was steady.

"We've uncovered somethin' far greater than we ever imagined," he began. "The Mormaer appeared tae me for a reason. I dinnae ken why yet—but I intend tae find out."

The others remained silent, caught in the weight of what they'd discovered. The room, warm just a moment ago, seemed to cool. Then, with a soft shimmer in the air, Elspeth appeared.

Her presence was gentle, but commanding. Silver hair trailing down her back, she stood in the centre of the hall, eyes glowing with quiet knowledge. Her gaze locked with Dougal's.

"Ye feel it, don't ye?" she said softly, her voice reverberating as though carried by the very stones. "The land calls tae ye, Dougal. The Mormaer saw it, as dae I. Ye've always had the sight. But now, ye've stepped fully into yer role."

Dougal swallowed. "Why me?"

"Because ye're meant tae guard it," she said, stepping closer. "Not just the land, but what lies beneath it. The wisdom. The memory. The truth of our people. This place chose ye. Ye heard it call, and ye answered."

She turned briefly, her gaze passing over each of them.

"Fiona, ye must be patient wi' the knowledge ye seek. It comes slowly but burns bright when lit. Angus, there will come a time for strength—but strength tempered wi' wisdom. Morag, your instincts will keep this group honest. Ye know when silence speaks louder than words. Ewan, remain steady, as ye always have. The others will need yer calm when storms rise. And Maree... your heart sees more than most. Keep it open, even when fear presses in."

Each name she spoke seemed to awaken something in them. Fiona's shoulders relaxed, her sharp eyes softening. Angus looked down, as if weighing the future in his palms. Morag's chin lifted with quiet pride, while Ewan gave a small nod, his jaw set in stoic readiness. Maree blinked hard, touched by the recognition of what she already knew in her bones—that heart, not heritage, was the measure of one's calling.

Maree moved to his side, placing a steadying hand on his arm. "Then we face it together, Dougal. This isn't just about bloodlines. It's about who's willin' tae stand. And we're all standin' wi' ye."

Angus leaned forward, expression hardening. "We need tae understand these scrolls. If there's knowledge here—military, agricultural, medicinal—we use it tae rebuild. Tae strengthen the estate."

"And tae protect it," added Ewan, his voice quiet but firm. "If this knowledge was hidden, there's likely a reason. We cannae be careless wi' it."

Fiona had already begun unrolling one of the scrolls, her eyes flicking quickly across the symbols and lines. "These are detailed maps. Not just of Clachanoch, but nearby lands. There's even symbols I've no' seen before... they could mark other strongholds."

She paused, reading a line aloud, her voice low and careful:

"...and when the circle is broken, the silence must be held, lest the fire awaken."

Morag stepped closer, her brow creased. "So what are we now? Keepers of history? Defenders o' secrets?"

Elspeth nodded slowly. "The Mormaer's men were guardians. Protectors. They built a network. A resistance. It was never just about defence. It was about preservation—of life, of identity, of spirit."

She turned her gaze once again to Dougal. "This task will test ye. There may be other guardians—others who've forgotten their purpose, or worse, corrupted it. Not all who seek this knowledge will be worthy of it."

There was a quiet murmur of agreement, but beneath it, the sense of something sacred was rising. The hall no longer felt like a room—it felt like a chamber of vows. In that moment, even the flicker of the fire seemed more intentional, as though bearing witness. They were no longer just residents of Clachanoch. They had become something more. A council. A fellowship bound by land and legacy.

Maree frowned, watching Dougal closely. "Ye're white as a ghost again, love. Sit down a moment."

He did, gratefully. The vision, the depth of it all—it had taken something from him. But he also felt it returning slowly. Like the land itself was breathing through him, steadying his pulse.

Elspeth's presence shimmered again, the room dimming as though time itself was holding its breath.

"What ye seek lies beyond the circle not of stone... but of soul," she said, her voice now distant, as if echoing through time. "The tunnels once ran with more than water. The land has not forgotten. Ye will need its forgiveness before ye walk freely." Dougal was struck. He'd heard those very words before.

The flames danced higher in the hearth, casting elongated shadows across the room. A wind swept faintly through the hall, though no door had opened.

Elspeth began to fade, her image growing translucent. "Guard it well, and ye will find the answers ye seek."

And then she was gone.

The silence that followed felt different than before—thicker, heavier, laced with the solemnity of a commission received. They were no longer searching for a purpose. It had found them. Each of them had felt it, even if no one spoke it aloud. Clachanoch had named them. And that kind of calling did not release its grip.

For a long moment, no one spoke.

Then Dougal stood, taller than he had before. His voice was low, but resolute. "We start by translatin' these scrolls. Piece by piece, we learn what the Mormaer and his kin tried tae pass down. We do it quietly. And we do it together."

Maree stepped in beside him. "Aye. Together."

Fiona gently rolled the scroll back up. "There's no time tae waste."

Angus let out a low breath. "And no room for mistakes."

Ewan nodded. "We keep this between us. For now. Until we know what we're dealin' with."

Morag folded her arms, casting a glance toward the shuttered windows. "We've been chosen for a reason. That means actin' wi' care."

Outside, the wind howled along the hills, wild and ancient. But within the manor, there was a stillness. A weight of purpose.

And as Dougal stared into the fire, the last words of the Mormaer echoed once more in his mind.

"Guard it well."

He whispered it aloud, the vow binding him as surely as any oath.

"Guard it well."

THE HIDDEN POWER

Despite all they had uncovered—the gold, the scrolls, the intricate network of tunnels—Dougal couldn't shake the feeling that something was still missing. The estate had been revealing its secrets in layers, each discovery leading them deeper into a history that had never been passed down to them. But why?

One evening, as they studied the newly drawn maps of the tunnels, Maree frowned at an odd marking near the farthest stretch of the underground passageways. It was subtle, barely there, but it didn't match anything else.

"Has anyone else noticed dis?" she asked, pointing to a section that seemed to end abruptly.

Fiona peered at it, then at the records they had compiled. "That path disnae lead anywhere—least not anywhere we know of."

"Aye, but look," Maree traced her finger along the tunnel's line, stopping at a tiny etching. A standin' stone.

Silence settled over them.

"A standin' stone?" Angus muttered. "Here? But we've never seen one on the property."

"That doesnae mean it isnae there," Dougal murmured. "It could've fallen, or been buried."

Maree's mind raced. "Dinnae ye see? If this tunnel leads tae a standin' stone... and the Doonigans have one at their croft..."

Fiona's breath hitched. "Then it means they were connected. All this time."

Ewan crossed his arms, his brow furrowed. "But if that's true, how come nane o' our forefathers knew about it? If these tunnels were built by the Mormaer, then why weren't they ever spoken about in McBeth history?"

A sobering thought settled over them.

Dougal exhaled slowly. "Because the McBeths never built them."

Morag's voice was quiet but certain. "And they never knew they existed."

A silence deeper than the one before followed, not awkward but reverent. It was as if even the walls held their breath, waiting for someone to finally speak the truth aloud. The ground beneath them had held generations of footsteps, yet none had truly seen what lay hidden. Now, it was awakening—and so were they.

That was the only explanation. The tunnels—the network, the hidden caches, the portal—had all been constructed long before their family ever took hold of Clachanoch. The Mormaer had built them, but the knowledge had died with him. The McBeths had lived above this labyrinth for centuries, completely unaware of what lay beneath their feet.

And now, that lost knowledge had found them.

Determined to find the hidden standing stone, the group ventured back underground, following the tunnel where the map had marked the peculiar symbol.

The passage was narrow and rough, unlike the main tunnels. The walls felt older, untouched by any McBeth hand. And as they walked, the air grew heavy, thick with something ancient.

Maree felt it first—a shift, a vibration in the stones beneath her fingertips.

"We're close," she murmured.

Then, Dougal's lantern flickered—not from lack of oil, but as if something unseen had passed through the flame.

And then they saw it.

A large, smooth stone, half-buried at the tunnel's end. Unlike the jagged rock surrounding it, this was deliberate—placed here with purpose. The same markings found on the Doonigan stones were faintly etched into its surface.

Fiona exhaled sharply. "Dat's no ordinary stone. That's a marker."

"Aye," Dougal agreed. "And it's been sealed away for a very long time."

The moment he reached out to touch it, the ground trembled—a deep, resonating vibration that seemed to hum through the very walls of the tunnel.

And then—a thin beam of light split through the cracks.

Maree gasped. "It's openin'."

A low groan of shifting rock echoed through the tunnel, dust spilling from above as the massive stone slowly moved, revealing a darkened passageway beyond.

Elspeth's voice came from the shadows. "Aye, lass. Ye found it."

They turned as she stepped into the dim lantern light, her expression one of quiet pride.

"So this is how ye travel," Dougal said, the realisation dawning. "This is how ye appear and disappear."

Elspeth nodded, running a hand along the stone as if greeting an old friend. "Not just me. Those before me. Those who protected what was meant tae be kept hidden."

Maree's breath caught. "It's a portal."

Elspeth met her gaze. "Aye. And it's been waitin' for ye."

A charged silence settled over them.

"If we go through," Angus said cautiously, "there's no tellin' what we'll find."

"Aye," Dougal agreed. "But we've come this far. There's no turnin' back now."

Fiona tightened her grip on the lantern, her knuckles white. "We're not just walkin' through stone—we're crossin' into memory. The land remembers. So must we." Her words weren't dramatic, just certain. They echoed in the passageway like a vow made by more than one voice.

With one last glance at each other, they stepped forward.

As the portal opened fully, the air shifted around them—history breathing once more, pulling them toward the unknown.

* * *

The air thickened as Dougal, Maree, Fiona, Angus, Ewan, and Morag stepped beyond the threshold of the newly opened passage. The tunnel ahead was unlike anything they had encountered before.

The walls were smooth, almost polished, as though the stone had been shaped by hands far older than their own ancestors. A faint, pulsing light traced along the edges of the passage—not torchlight, nor moonlight, but something different.

Dougal squinted into the dim beyond. Just for a moment, he thought he saw the shadow of a tall tower in the distance—half-formed, like a memory trying to surface. He blinked, and it was gone.

"It's as if the walls themselves remember," Fiona whispered.

"Or they're guidin' us," Ewan muttered, running his hand along the carved surface.

Elspeth stepped forward, her gaze filled with both familiarity and reverence. "This path has been sealed for centuries, yet it knows ye belong here. That means ye are ready."

"Ready for what?" Dougal asked.

Elspeth studied him for a long moment before answering. "Tae learn the truth o' Clachanoch."

The passage eventually opened into a vast chamber, its ceiling so high that their lantern light barely touched the edges. Stones stood in a circular formation at its centre—not crude or broken, but deliberately placed, carefully measured.

And then, in the dim light, they saw it.

An ancient emblem, carved deep into the largest of the stones. The same emblem they had seen on the scrolls, on the maps, and at the Doonigan's croft.

Maree stepped forward first, something drawing her in.

"This is it," she whispered.

A rush of cool air swept through the chamber—not from outside, but from within the stone circle itself.

And then, without warning—the light shifted.

Where once there was empty space, now there was something else.

A doorway.

Not carved, nor built, nor forced into the rock, but created of nothingness, a thin veil between what was and what had been.

Elspeth exhaled, her voice thick with emotion. "Aye. The portal still lives."

Dougal's heart pounded. He had seen many strange things since returning to Clachanoch, but this? This defied all reason.

"How is this possible?" Morag breathed.

But even as she asked it, she staggered slightly—her eyes glassing over, hand reaching for the nearest stone as though it could steady the storm within her.

Maree moved quickly to her side. "Morag! What is it?"

Morag didn't answer right away. She stared at the emblem, and a single tear rolled down her cheek.

"I dinnae know," she whispered. "But I feel like I've stood here before."

"Because it was never meant tae be lost," Elspeth answered.

She turned to them, eyes bright. "Listen tae me now, for ye need tae ken the truth before ye step through. This is nae a passage tae another world, nor is it magic. It is a key. A key tae the past, tae memories locked away. And if ye enter, ye will see what the Mormaer wished ye tae see."

"See what?" Dougal asked.

Elspeth stepped toward the glowing veil and gestured. "The fall o' Clachanoch."

Silence.

"The fall?" Angus repeated. "I thought the estate always belonged tae our family?"

Elspeth's eyes darkened. "That is what ye were told. But history doesnae always belong tae the victors—sometimes, it is simply forgotten. The McBeths took this land, aye, but they were not its first keepers. And the Mormaer... he did not die as ye were led tae believe."

No one moved. The truth pressed down like mist over moorland, settling in their lungs, heavier than the stone around them. A history rewritten, a legacy inherited under false light. And now, standing at the edge of revelation, there was no turning away.

The weight of her words settled like stone.

Fiona inhaled sharply. "Then what happened?"

Elspeth held out a hand toward the portal. "Step through, and ye will see."

Maree was the first to move. Without hesitation, she stepped forward, into the veiled light.

And one by one, they followed.

The moment they crossed, the chamber dissolved around them—and time itself shifted.

The air smelled different. Fresher. Alive.

When Dougal's eyes adjusted, he realized they were no longer standing in the hidden chamber.

They were outside.

The hills of Clachanoch stretched before them, but the land was not as they had known it. The manor was nowhere in sight. Instead, a great stone keep stood in its place, its towers unbroken, its walls intact.

And beyond it, men rode on horseback, banners flying, armour gleaming in the light of a long-dead sun.

"By the saints," Ewan breathed. "We've stepped into the past."

A horn sounded in the distance, and suddenly, the ground shook beneath them.

War was coming.

And in the faces of the approaching riders, Dougal thought he glimpsed something terrifyingly familiar—his own brow, his own eyes, reflected in warriors long gone. They hadn't just returned to witness history. They were about to walk inside it.

And as the thunder of hooves approached from the hills, they realised they weren't just here to witness history—

They were part of it.

ECHOES OF THE FALLEN

The clang of steel rang through the air, the sound of clashing swords and battle cries cutting through the rolling hills of Clachanoch.

Dougal, Maree, Fiona, Angus, Ewan, and Morag stood frozen, watching the past unfold before their eyes.

The Mormaer's forces were locked in combat against an invading force—men clad in darkened armour, their banners unfamiliar, their war cries foreign.

"Norse," Angus whispered, his voice tight with disbelief. "We've heard stories o' the raids, but this... this is it."

"Nae just a raid," Fiona muttered, her gaze sweeping across the battlefield. "This is a siege."

The great stone keep, once standing proud upon the land, was under attack.

And they were standing in the middle of it.

As they watched, the Mormaer of Moray appeared atop the ramparts, his voice booming over the battlefield.

"Hold fast, men! We fight for our land, our kin, and our blood! Do not falter!"

A chorus of cheers erupted from the warriors behind him. But even as the Mormaer stood strong, Dougal could see the grim determination in his face.

"He kens they willnae win this fight," Dougal murmured.

Maree's breath hitched. "Then this is where it happened. Where it all changed."

Below, the invaders surged forward, ladders slamming against the keep's walls. Flaming arrows streaked through the sky, setting wooden defences alight. The scent of smoke, sweat, and blood thickened in the air.

And then, with a deafening crack, the eastern gate buckled.

The enemy poured in.

The heat of fire met the cold sting of betrayal in the wind, a strange collision of elements that made Maree step back as though scorched. None of them could move. Not even to breathe deeply. It was no longer simply witnessing a battle—it was stepping into the death throes of a kingdom that once was their own, in blood if not in right.

"We should do somethin'!" Morag blurted, stepping forward—only for Elspeth to grip her wrist, holding her back.

"Nay, lass," Elspeth said firmly, her eyes filled with sorrow. "Ye cannae change what has already come tae pass."

Morag swallowed hard, fists clenching helplessly. A raw sob caught in her throat. She didn't ken why it hit her so hard—but something inside her broke as the Mormaer fell.

Because she knew Elspeth was right.

They were not here to fight. They were here to witness.

Dougal turned his attention away from the battle—to the shadows behind the keep's walls.

Men moved swiftly, deliberately.

Not Norse. Not invaders. Scottish.

"Who are they?" Ewan frowned. "They arenae fightin'—they're... sneakin'."

And then, Dougal saw it.

One of them—a man draped in darkened plaid, his face obscured—reached for the iron-wrought gate leading to the tunnels.

And unlocked it.

"Nay," Dougal whispered, his stomach twisting. "This was an inside job."

Angus's expression darkened. "Someone betrayed the Mormaer."

The hidden tunnels, once built to preserve and protect, had been turned against them.

Maree took a step closer, her voice hollow. "Then Clachanoch didnae fall... it was handed over."

As the Mormaer's forces were slaughtered in the court-yard, their leader cut down on the steps of his own keep, the truth settled over them like a death knell.

In the final moments before the vision faded, Dougal saw the Mormaer's gaze shift—not to the enemy, but toward the open gate. Not fear. Not even pain. Just recognition. He had known. He had died knowing. And Dougal felt that knowing burn its way into his soul, as if it were now his burden to carry.

Then—darkness.

The world rippled, the battlefield fading into shadow, the screams dissolving into echoes.

And in the blink of an eye, they were back.

The chamber beneath the estate surrounded them once more, the portal's glow fading into nothingness.

A raw sob caught in her throat. She didn't ken why it hit her so hard—but something inside her broke as the Mormaer fell.

For a long moment, no one spoke.

Then Fiona exhaled, hands shaking. "We've been lied tae for generations."

"This land," Morag whispered. "This estate—it wasnae always ours. It felt like losin' my own. Like I'd lived it before."

Dougal glanced toward the space where the tower had shimmered—still echoing in his mind like a ghost half-remembered.

He swallowed the lump in his throat, his mind racing.

Everything they thought they knew about Clachanoch had been a lie.

And now, they had to decide what to do with the truth.

* * *

The silence in the chamber was thick, pressing in on them as they processed what they had just witnessed.

The Mormaer had not fallen by sheer force alone.

He had been betrayed.

And someone—one of their own people—had unlocked the gate that sealed his fate.

Dougal paced, raking a hand through his hair, his mind reeling. "We always thought Clachanoch was ours by right—ours tae reclaim, tae restore."

Maree's face was pale, her voice hollow. "But if it was taken through treachery... then what does that make us?"

Fiona crossed her arms tightly, her gaze stormy. "I'll tell ye what it makes us—descendants o' the wrong side."

Ewan muttered a curse under his breath. Angus, ever the pragmatic one, simply exhaled sharply, shaking his head.

"If this was an inside job," Angus said, "there has tae be a record o' it somewhere."

"Aye," Dougal agreed, his pulse pounding. "And if anyone kens the truth, it'll be in these tunnels."

A new mission had formed.

They had uncovered how Clachanoch had fallen.

Now they had to uncover who had let it happen.

They spread out, each of them scanning the forgotten war room beneath the estate with new eyes.

Maree moved without speaking, her hand brushing every stone as if expecting it to respond. She needed to feel something solid—anything to ground her from the nausea rising in her chest. It wasn't just the truth that had shaken her. It was the realisation that generations had lived and died clinging to a story built on another man's betrayal.

The Mormaer's final battle plans still lay upon the great wooden table, now weathered with time, but Dougal's focus was elsewhere.

He ran his fingers over the shelves carved into the stone, their contents long undisturbed. Most contained battle maps, old military strategies, and treaties—until his hand brushed against something different.

A sealed leather ledger.

A name scrawled on its cover in faded ink.

"Tavish McBeth."

A chill raced down Dougal's spine.

"McBeth."

He turned slowly, holding up the ledger. "I think I've found our traitor."

Maree's breath caught. "Nay."

Fiona snatched the book from his hands, flipping through the brittle pages, her face darkening with every entry.

"By the gods..." she murmured.

Dougal peered over her shoulder.

The pages were detailed accounts of meetings, correspondence, and movements.

Tavish McBeth had been negotiating with the enemy.

Selling secrets. Undermining the Mormaer.

And in the final entry, dated the very night Clachanoch fell, his guilt was laid bare:

"The gate is unbarred. The Norse will do the rest."

A wave of nausea rolled through Dougal. "He sold them out. He sold out his own people."

Maree shook her head furiously. "But why? Why would one of our ancestors betray the Mormaer?"

"Greed," Ewan spat. "Power. A promise o' survival."

Angus leaned against the table, his jaw clenched. "So Clachanoch was never rightfully ours."

A heavy silence settled over them.

Their entire lineage, their entire claim to this land, had been built on a lie.

And now, they were the ones who had to reckon with it.

Fiona closed the ledger and stared into the hearth. "How many o' yer kin boasted about reclaimin' this place?" she asked quietly. "As if it were their birthright. As if no blood had been spilt beneath the stones. What fools we've been… and what price they paid."

Elspeth's voice broke the silence.

"The past doesnae bind ye, Dougal McBeth."

They turned.

She stood at the edge of the chamber, her ethereal presence shimmering like candlelight.

"What was stolen can be restored. What was broken can be mended. But ye must decide—will ye bear the weight of Tavish McBeth's betrayal, or will ye forge a new legacy?"

Dougal swallowed hard, his pulse thundering in his ears.

Maree's eyes searched his face, waiting.

The decision lay with him.

With them.

Would they walk away?

Or would they make things right?

Dougal looked down at the ledger—the confession of their ancestor's treachery.

Then, with steely resolve, he decided not to toss it into the fire.

The flames roared higher beckoning him to change his mind.

"The truth was buried," he said quietly. "And so were the people who tried tae protect it."

He looked up, meeting each of their eyes.

"We are McBeths," Dougal said, his voice unwavering. "And we will restore what was lost."

The chamber seemed to breathe around them, the weight of history finally shifting.

The past had spoken.

Now, it was their turn.

THE WEIGHT OF HISTORY

The chamber's silence lingered long after Elspeth's words had faded, each of them grappling with the weight of what they had just uncovered. Tavish Mc-Beth—an ancestor, a traitor. A man who had bartered away the Mormaer's trust, and in doing so, condemned Clachanoch to centuries of falsehood.

Dougal sat heavily on the edge of the old war table, the ledger still in his hands, the brittle parchment whispering treachery. The others remained close—Fiona pacing, Angus and Ewan leaning silently against the stone walls, Maree and Morag sharing a look heavy with questions. The faint flicker of torchlight threw uncertain shadows across their faces.

"How dae we bear this?" Dougal murmured. "How dae we claim this land as ours, knowin' it was taken through treachery?"

No one answered at first.

Elspeth finally stepped forward, her voice low and steady. "The past is written, aye. But the story ye tell from it is yet yers tae shape. Tavish made his choices. His legacy need not be yers."

Maree wrapped her shawl tighter around her shoulders. "Aye, but will the village see it that way? They'll question why this truth was hidden for so long. Why no one before us sought tae bring it tae light."

Fiona stopped pacing and turned, eyes sharp. "Then we show them. We tell 'em the truth, openly. No' just tae clear our own conscience, but tae restore what was lost."

"Is it that simple?" Ewan asked, his voice laced with doubt. "Truth has weight. And this truth... it'll land hard."

Angus crossed his arms. "Aye. Especially if folk believe we only found it tae serve ourselves."

Morag shifted uncomfortably. She had said little since the vision. Her normally steady gaze was troubled, distant. Finally, she spoke.

"I felt somethin' when we crossed that veil," she said, almost to herself. "Like I belonged there—but not wi' them."

Maree frowned. "What do ye mean?"

Morag lifted her chin, meeting their eyes. "Those Norsemen. Their hair. Their skin. Their eyes. I saw my own reflection in theirs. I think... I think I'm one o' them. Not McBeth. Not Highlander. But somethin' older. Somethin' long lost."

The revelation drew silence. Not of shock, but understanding.

Ewan moved to her side without a word. She took comfort in his closeness, though her eyes stayed locked on the flickering flames.

In that moment, something shifted—not just in Morag, but in them all. The story of Clachanoch no longer belonged to one bloodline, one clan, or even one truth. It was a tapestry of voices long silenced, now slowly rising again. And Morag's words, though simple, had cracked something wide open.

Dougal stood, finally breaking the quiet. "We need tae think this through. Talk tae someone wi' perspective. We're standin' in the bones o' history—but that doesn't mean we're the ones tae rewrite it."

Elspeth nodded. "There is wisdom in patience. There is power in counsel."

"Old Mr. Campbell," Fiona said. "He's always had a foot in both worlds—history and community."

Dougal gave a slow nod. "Aye. We start there."

The next morning, the group welcomed Mr. Campbell into the study at Clachanoch. The old historian, wrapped in his brown wool coat and still spry despite the stoop in his shoulders, examined the scrolls and the ledger with care. When he finally spoke, his words were slow and deliberate.

"This changes things," he said. "And no' just for you, but for the village. For this land."

"But should we share it all?" Maree asked. "Will it heal... or divide?"

Campbell studied her, then looked to Morag. "Lass, ye said ye felt kin tae those Norse folk?"

Morag hesitated. "Aye. It's in me blood. I felt it like a pulse."

Campbell smiled gently. "Then it means yer voice matters even more. If we're tae make peace wi' the past, we need tae own every part of it. No shame. No silence."

Angus sighed. "And if the villagers fight us on it?"

"Then ye listen," Campbell replied. "Then ye tell 'em why it matters. Truth can sting. But it also sets things right."

Dougal nodded slowly. "Then we prepare."

Maree placed a hand on his arm. "One step at a time. Let's think this through. Honour the Mormaer. Show the betrayal, aye—but also the courage. The resistance. The survival."

Elspeth, who had been silent, added one final thought. "And show them you've changed the story. That yer legacy starts now, no' with Tavish."

Mr. Campbell tapped the ledger lightly, then placed a weathered hand over it. "History's no just written wi' ink," he said. "It's written wi' action. Wi' humility. Ye can't undo the past, but ye can choose whether ye live under its shadow—or rise above it." The firelight glinted in his eyes as he added, "And I believe ye're the ones tae rise."

Dougal met each of their eyes. "We open the doors. But we do it on our terms. Together."

That night, Clachanoch stood quiet, the candlelight glowing from its windows like beacons on the hill. Within, the group gathered again around the hearth. The fire snapped softly, casting warmth across tired faces.

They had chosen their path.

But what lay beyond it, only the truth would tell.

Maree stared into the flames, her hand unconsciously resting atop Dougal's. "We thought we came tae fix a roof... and instead, we've uncovered a nation's wound." Her words were quiet, not heavy—but honest. Around her, the others nodded in silent agreement. This was no longer just about restoration. It was redemption.

And when the doors opened next, it would not be as the keepers of secrets—but as the keepers of Clachanoch's truth.

CHAPTER

28

RECKONING DAY

The morning of the gathering dawned grey and wind-stirred, as though the Highlands themselves sensed what was coming. Clachanoch's great hall had been prepared with care—benches set in rows, trestle tables laden with relics, maps pinned to boards. The scrolls remained protected, but faithful reproductions were laid out for the villagers to study.

The McBeths stood together at the head of the room—Dougal, Maree, Fiona, Angus, Ewan, and Morag—a united front, though each carried their own nerves. Today, they would reveal everything: the betrayal, the truth of Tavish McBeth, the role of the Mormaer, and the tunnels that snaked beneath their feet like veins through the land.

The walls, once cold with silence, now bore the echoes of footsteps and the shuffling of chairs. It felt like standing before a judgment—not just of people, but of time itself. The great hall, so often empty, now carried the breath of generations who had never known the truth.

The villagers filed in slowly. Old Mr. Campbell arrived first, spectacles already perched on his nose. Behind him came Isla Fraser and her daughters, then John the butcher, followed by the barkeep Donald MacCrae and his formidable wife, Jean. More followed—farmers, shopkeepers, even a few sceptics who rarely left their crofts. There was curiosity, apprehension, even suspicion in the air.

Dougal stepped forward.

"Thank ye all for comin'," he began, his voice firm but solemn. "Today's no' just about Clachanoch. It's about all of us. About this land. Its history. And the truths that were hidden for far too long."

He gestured to the display table. Fiona stepped in, beginning the presentation. She spoke clearly, her scholarly tone grounding what might have otherwise felt unbelievable.

But as the ledger of Tavish McBeth was introduced, the room's atmosphere shifted.

Murmurs rose.

"What's this about betrayal?" someone barked.

Jean MacCrae stepped forward, squinting at the old ink. "Are ye sayin' one o' yer own sold out the Mormaer?"

"Aye," Dougal said. "Tavish McBeth. He let the Norse invaders in. The Mormaer and his men were slaughtered because o' him. And this land... it passed to the McBeths after that."

A roar went up.

"So ye admit ye're livin' in a stolen keep?" shouted Malcolm Reid, his face flushed red.

"We dinnae know until recently," Maree interjected, stepping forward. "We found the truth buried in the tunnels. In Tavish's own hand."

"So now ye expect us tae clap for ye?" Jean MacCrae snapped. "Tae thank ye for sharin'?"

For a breath, it seemed the entire room hung in that moment—old anger bristling against new honesty. And yet behind the tension, something deeper stirred. The villagers weren't just reacting to the truth. They were confronting the stories they'd always believed. And that, too, was a kind of grief.

Morag, her voice calm but intense, cut through the noise. "We're no' askin' for thanks. We're offerin' the truth. And a choice."

The room quieted.

"There's more," she continued. "This betrayal—it doesnae define what came after. The McBeths, whether knowingly or no', preserved this land. And now, we've a chance tae do right by it."

Old Mr. Campbell raised a trembling hand. "Let's hear what else they found."

Maps were explained—routes leading to other ancient sites, the network of resistance. The community leaned in again. Curiosity began to edge out hostility.

Still, doubts lingered.

Donald MacCrae cleared his throat. "Aye, it's a fine story. But why share it now? Ye could've kept it all. Claimed it was McBeth glory."

Dougal looked around the room. "Because we're tired o' secrets. Because this estate should serve the community again. We want tae work wi' ye. Rebuild what was meant tae be shared."

There was a long pause.

Then, slowly, Angus spoke. "We're namin' the rooms after the fallen clans. Dedicatin' one tae the Mormaer himself."

Fiona added, "And we'll be workin' with Mr Campbell tae build a permanent archive—open tae all."

Stillness.

Then Morag, who had remained uncharacteristically quiet until now, took a step forward.

"I saw the battle," she said softly. "Felt it. And I know this blood runs in me, too. But it's nae about claimin' sides anymore. It's about what we choose tae carry forward."

Ewan looked to her, heart swelling with quiet pride. It was Morag's words, so grounded and stripped of pretence, that landed where other speeches could not. She had seen the truth not with her eyes—but with her bones. And the people could feel that.

Her eyes scanned the villagers—some wide-eyed, some ashamed, some still bristling.

"We dinnae rewrite what happened. But we make sure it's no' forgotten."

Old Mr. Campbell nodded slowly. "Then maybe it's time we stop guardin' ghosts, and start honourin' 'em."

A slow clap echoed from the back. Then another. Until the hall once more rang with the sound of hands—not just in politeness, but in recognition.

Outside, the sun broke through the clouds.

Inside, a reckoning had begun—not just for the McBeths, but for everyone.

The story had changed.

And Clachanoch was no longer a house divided by shadows.

It was a land opening its arms—finally—to truth.

EPILOGUE

History Meets Destiny

With the major repairs complete, Clachanoch Estate was no longer a crumbling relic of the past. It had become something else entirely—a place of discovery, renewal, and hope. The house now stood proud, its towering stone walls sturdy once more, its grand halls no longer filled with decay but with the promise of a new era.

It had been Maree's idea, initially spoken in passing as they sat by the fire one evening. "Ye ken," she had mused, swirling the last of her whisky in her glass, "there's somethin' special about this place. Folk would come far an' wide tae stay in a house wi' such history."

The idea took root, and soon, they were making plans.

"Aye," Dougal agreed. "With at least twenty grand rooms and the same amount of smaller ones, we could turn it into a proper bed and breakfast. Offer people a chance tae experience Clachanoch, its history, its beauty."

"We could even incorporate the tunnels," Angus added, his brow furrowed in thought. "Guided tours through the chambers, showin' the hidden passages, the war room, all of it. The world needs tae ken what happened here."

Fiona nodded. "And that's the point—tae tell the truth. No the half-truths passed down, but the real history, wi' evidence tae prove it. The community deserves that much."

In the weeks that followed, locals began to offer their help—some donating heirlooms, others lending their time or skills. What had once divided them now bound them together. It was no longer the McBeths' burden to bear, but a shared legacy—one they all now claimed with cautious pride.

Opening Clachanoch's doors to guests was one thing, but the greater task lay in restoring the historical narrative. The tunnels beneath the estate had unveiled a hidden chapter of Scotland's past, proving that the Mormaer and his people had built more than just a noble home—they had established a stronghold, a sanctuary, a place where knowledge and resistance had been preserved in the face of war.

Word had already spread through the village, and the people of the surrounding lands were eager to hear the full story. It was their history, too.

A gathering was planned in the great hall—one of the first of many to come. The group carefully arranged the relics, maps, and scrolls that had been unearthed, presenting them as irrefutable evidence of the Mormaer's legacy. The local historian, old Mr Campbell, was nearly beside himself with excitement, calling it "a revelation tae Scotland's history."

"We've all been livin' on land we barely understood," he told the crowd. "Clachanoch was at the heart o' something far greater than we ever imagined. This estate is more than bricks an' mortar—it's a bridge tae our past."

Morag, standing near the display of artefacts, stepped forward with a quiet kind of authority. "And maybe," she murmured, "it's also a bridge tae our future."

There was no applause—just a hush of reverence. In that silence was something stronger than praise: agreement. A shared knowing that they stood not only among stones and scrolls, but among the echoes of those who had once stood and fought, built and hoped, just as they did now.

She felt the words in her bones.

Ever since their journey through the portal, she'd been coming to terms with what she had seen—and what she had felt. That tug in her chest, the strange recognition in the eyes of the fallen Norsemen, the heavy sense of loss and purpose that had washed over her as they watched the siege.

She knew now.

She descended from them.

She wasn't just part of Clachanoch's future—she was a piece of its forgotten past.

A month later, Clachanoch's chapel stood transformed. Once abandoned and in ruins, it now gleamed with new stained-glass windows, its stone walls restored, its pews repaired by the very hands of those who would gather there.

The occasion? Fiona and Angus's wedding.

The ceremony was simple but deeply meaningful. Fiona, ever pragmatic, had scoffed at the idea of an extravagant affair, but Maree and Morag had insisted on at least a touch of elegance. As Fiona stood at the altar in a gown of deep blue—a nod to her homeland—there was a softness to her that few had seen before.

Angus, standing tall and proud in his formal Highland attire, could not take his eyes off her. "Ye look like the sunrise o'er the hills, lass," he whispered, causing Fiona to blush fiercely.

As the vows were exchanged, Clachanoch itself seemed to exhale, as if the old house knew that it was witnessing something that had been a long time coming—a union not just of two people, but of history and future, of past wounds and new hope.

Children ran barefoot across the grass that night, lanterns swaying in their hands. Old songs were sung, new laughter echoed off the walls, and the memory of grief was, for a time, replaced with joy. In the eyes of those who danced, history found healing—not in forgetting, but in honouring.

The celebration stretched well into the night. Music filled the halls, laughter echoed through the once-empty corridors, and glasses were raised in endless toasts. Clachanoch was alive again.

Amid the revelry, Morag stood quietly near one of the newly installed windows, watching the moonlight spill over the grounds. Her fair hair caught the glow, almost silver in the night. It was something she had always been aware of—her lighter hair, her blue-green eyes, her delicate features that set her apart.

Now, she understood why.

Her ancestry wasn't just a curiosity—it was a key.

She turned to Maree, who had come to stand beside her.

"I ken now," Morag said softly. "The reason I've always felt different. I saw it, Maree. In the past. In the eyes o' those men fightin' for their land. I felt it when the portal opened. I come from them. The Norse."

Maree nodded, emotion thick in her throat. "And that means your journey's only just begun."

Morag's gaze drifted toward the distant hills, as though searching for something beyond sight.

And maybe she was.

Behind them, the music swelled again. But Morag remained still, a sentinel of memory, her heart stretched across time. Something in the air whispered of unfinished stories—paths yet to walk, names yet to uncover, truths waiting to rise from the soil like wildflowers.

The past had left its mark on Clachanoch.

And in Morag's blood, it still lived.

The next chapter, it seemed, belonged to her.

ALSO BY DEE WHITMAN

Whispers of the Highland Moors, Book One: *Heirs of the Highland*

Guardians of Clachanoch, Book Two: *Heirs of the Highland*

Legacy of the Lost Clans, Book Three: *Heirs of the Highland*

The Frontier Dance
The Frontier Christmas - *Coming Soon!*
The Frontier Reckoning - *Coming Soon!*

Calling of the Ancients

Lord Ashton's Enchantment - *Coming Soon!*